A Father for Christmas

A Veteran's Christmas # 1

Rachelle Ayala

Amiga Brook Press

>>><<<

"Heartwarming story of hope and second chances."
– Ruth Davis

"Absolutely breathtaking love story."
– Amber McCallister

ISBN-13: 978-1502474162
ISBN-10: 1502474166

Contact Rachelle at
http://rachelleayala.me/author-bio/contact/

>>><<<

Dedication

To all the veterans who gave so much.

Chapter 1

~ Kelly ~

"I WANT A PAPA FOR Christmas," my four-year-old daughter, Bree, tells Santa. She bounces in his lap and tugs his beard. "A real live papa to play with me and take me to the zoo."

"You mean a puppy," I cut in, my face flushed with heat. Ever since I put Bree in preschool, she's realized she's missing a father and bugging me to find one. She even suggested we put up posters on telephone poles like they do for lost pets.

"No, silly mama." Bree crosses her arms and shakes her blond ringlet curls. "I want a papa with two legs and two hands."

The mall-supplied Santa chuckles. "Ho, ho, ho. And a papa you shall have."

Giggles and titters spill from the women behind me.

"I need me one of those, too," a young mother holding a baby boy says. "Let's see, six-foot-six, blazing hot and built like a fire truck."

"Oh, yeah," another mother with two squirmy toddlers replies. "Do they have a catalog? I can spend hours drooling instead of wiping up drool."

Much like the hours I spent perusing anonymous sperm donor profiles back when I was a successful investment banker worried about aging eggs and the probability of getting struck by lightning without hitting the husband jackpot.

Bree hugs Santa. "Will he be under the tree? Pwo-mise?"

"You bet." Santa high fives her.

"Picture?" I scramble with my camera, an old Canon point-and-shoot borrowed from my mother, but the battery light flashes and the camera shuts off. Meanwhile, the elf manning the professional camera snaps a few shots of my sweet daughter kissing Santa. Ugh, I wonder how many germs are embedded in that polyester beard?

Santa hands Bree to me and winks. "Shall I put a smartphone under the tree for you?"

I'll need a lot more than a smartphone: try rent, utilities, and car payments. Not only was I a former investment banker, I was stupid enough to believe my own research and ended up losing everything on a bad tip.

"No, she wants a papa, too." Bree tugs my coat sleeve. "I hear her praying for one every night."

Thankfully, Santa doesn't answer. He's already receiving the baby from the woman behind me. And actually, no, I'm not praying for a man, but Bree hears what she wants to hear, and in her little mind, all of our problems will be solved when the handsome princely father figure emerges to sweep her off her feet in a cotton candy sleigh drawn by a team of rainbow reindeer.

As for me, I'll settle for responsible, solvent, and well-endowed, although in my profession, er, former profession, I never saw a need for a man, especially the banking types who kept half the strip clubs in Manhattan in business. No thank you.

The picture-taking elf smirks at me and hands me a ticket for the picture. "It'll be twenty bucks for a five-by-seven or thirty-five for the package."

"I want a train ride." Bree squirms from my arms and points to the Holiday Express miniature train making the rounds inside the enclosed winter wonderland play area in the mall. "When my papa shows up, he'll take me on the train and we can wave at you."

Clutching the ticket for Bree's picture with Santa, I bypass the photo booth conveniently placed near the line for the Holiday Express train. My meager paycheck has to be stretched for the holiday season, the first one since my insider trading conviction. Unable to land a job anywhere close to the financial services industry, I've been picking up shifts after-hours, cleaning the very office buildings I'm not allowed to enter as a banker.

But I can afford five dollars for a ride on the Holiday Express. Bree looks at me expectantly and points to the monitor behind the cash register. "Mommy, there's my picture with Santa."

"There you are, and don't you look cute?" I say, dreading her next request to buy it.

The cashier flashes a toothy smile. "We can have it printed while you wait for the Holiday Express."

"Can we?" Bree bounces on her toes. "He pwo-mised me a papa for Christmas."

"Maybe after the train, sweetie." Going for distraction over chancing a meltdown, I hand the cashier a ten dollar bill for our two tickets.

Fortunately, the screen behind her cycles to a baby boy crying on Santa's lap, and Bree's attention turns to the man selling candy canes.

"Mommy, candy cane's my fa-wor-ite."

"We have some at home."

"Those are teeny tiny. I want a big red and green one."

"We can't lose our place in line. Oh, look, see the fairy princesses?" I direct her toward three teenaged girls wearing princess outfits.

"They're so pretty." Bree's mesmerized, and I breathe easier. My phone chimes with a text message. I flip it open. It's my mother reminding me to be on time for Wednesday night church. We're singing a special together, and she wants to rehearse before the service.

The line inches forward as I text her back. Mama's nervous about the piano at church not responding like hers. Could I get to church half an hour early to do a dress rehearsal? I'm not sure why she's so nervous. Maybe it has to do with the handsome widower who recently joined the congregation. I tell her I still have to finish shopping and prepare dinner for Bree, but mother says that's not a problem. She'll bring macaroni and cheese and juice boxes to church, and Bree can eat in the multipurpose room. I agree, and Mama replies with her classic line to give Bree a kiss from her.

I text my goodbye and put my phone away. "Bree, Nana's giving you a kiss."

She's not standing anywhere near me. A hot dagger of panic shoots up my chest. "Bree? Oh no, where's Bree?"

She was here a minute ago. The line hadn't gone forward by much. Surely, she surged ahead to gawk at the train and the princesses. I jump out of line, looking toward the fairy princesses.

"Bree!" My voice rises to a high-pitched shriek. People are staring, and I'm running in circles. "Have you seen my daughter? Bree! Blonde, wearing a pink Hello Kitty jacket. Bree!"

I rush headlong to the picket fence separating the train tracks. What if she's on the tracks? "Stop the train. My daughter's missing."

A uniformed security guard heads toward me. "What seems to be the problem?"

"My daughter's missing. She was right here, and now she's gone. Bree!" My arms flail, and I tear through the line.

"I need a description." The guard corners me. "Height, weight, what she was wearing."

"She's four years old. Name's Bree Kennedy. Curly blond hair, I don't know, maybe forty pounds and three-and-a-half feet tall." My heart pounds in my chest. "We have to find her."

"We're trying, ma'am." He calls into his walkie-talkie. "Missing child. Four-year-old girl. Blonde. Answers to Bree."

"She was wearing a pink jacket and blue jeans. Dora the Explorer shoes," I add.

The guard reports into his device, then turns to me. "Why don't you come to the security office? Maybe someone's turned her in."

"No, I want to keep looking." My eyes are scanning the crowd. "I can't believe I lost her."

"It'll be okay." He hands me his card. "Give me your number so we can call you."

I hastily give my number and tuck the card into my purse. Wiping my eyes and trying hard to keep under control, I run around the train ride and check the line of children waiting for Santa. No Bree. No where.

"Have you seen my daughter? Blond hair, blue eyes? Four-year-old?" I'm frantically tapping people's shoulders. A middle-aged man and his wife join me on my search.

"It shouldn't be hard to spot a blonde," he says as his wife nods.

He's right. My daughter stands out at her preschool where the vast majority of children are ethnic Chinese, East Indian, or Hispanic. I'd noticed that earlier this year when we moved to the San Francisco Bay Area to be close to my mother after I was released from prison.

"What am I going to do?" I wail, my heart galloping with fright. "Bree! Where are you? Mommy's looking for you."

So many children and parents mill around, making it hard to spot a little girl on her own. Sympathetic faces turn to me and people murmur. The guard returns to my side and shrugs. "No sign of her. We've called the police. Do you have a photograph?"

My legs weaken and I stagger, dropping my purse on the floor. I turn it upside down and scramble through it for my photo wallet. Fat tears drop on my hands.

"Here, here." My fingers tremble as I give him the wallet-sized photo taken last year back in New York City with the Macy's Santa Claus.

"We've put out a lost child alert to all of the guards and merchants. Every exit has a camera, so if anyone tries to take her out, we'll have it recorded." The guard attempts to reassure me.

"What if someone's taken her to a restroom? What if they're hurting her?" Sharp pains pierce my gut as I push away horrifying thoughts. "My baby. Oh, God, please bring her back."

"We're checking all the restrooms and notified all the stores already," the guard says. "Please, come to the security office. The police will meet us there."

I shove my things into my purse and stumble after him, crying uncontrollably. "God, please, God. Help me find Bree. Oh, Bree, where are you?"

Chapter 2

~ Tyler ~

TYLER MANNING STROLLED THROUGH A coffee shop at the mall and scored a half-filled cup of coffee from a recently vacated bistro table. Still warm and black. He wiped the lipstick off the rim with a napkin and took a sip before adding a packet of sugar.

Being homeless and without a steady job meant he had to be on the lookout for leftovers. The pickings were good today.

It was two weeks before Christmas and shoppers were out in force. Canned Christmas music piped through the sound system, and a giant, eighty-foot Christmas tree was erected under the stained glass dome of the mall. Every arch was festooned with multi-colored strobe lights, and a dazzling amount of golden ornaments and fake snow decorated the windows.

Christmas season. A time of fake cheer and phony laughter. Just another excuse for businesses to bleed people dry. Especially during the worst recession he'd seen since returning from Afghanistan.

Tyler's hands shook as he tipped the coffee cup to his lips. Here he was, back in a country where people had their heads up their asses, unconcerned and ungrateful to chumps like him who'd believed the rhetoric and put their miserable lives on the line.

Ten years ago, he'd left his hometown a hero, quarterback of his college football team and a draft pick to play pro ball. He'd given it all up for a chance to serve his country, to fight for freedom and protect his homeland. Now? He was a big zero. A head case, hearing roadside bombs and men's screams in his head, haunted by the internal movie of buddies dead and missions failed.

Tyler wandered among the shoppers, almost tripping over a small boy clutching a toy fire truck as if the sum of all happiness resided in that piece of plastic, made in China. The boy's mother grabbed her son's hand and shot Tyler a suspicious glare. Guess letting his hair and beard grow while wearing cast off clothes from a veteran's charity was too much of a contrast to the upper crust folks at this upscale mall so close to the San Francisco Financial District.

He could walk around here if he wanted to. There was no better place to scrounge food than at an affluent shopping center where women watched their waistlines and picky children limited themselves to a single food group. Since the customers here were accustomed to maids picking up for them, they oftentimes left entire plates of food on the table without throwing their leftovers into the trash or busing their own trays. As long as he didn't look too much like a bum, he could simply sit down at the table and pretend he'd gone to get a napkin or several packets of ketchup before returning to his meal.

Most people had their noses too far in the air to care, so besotted were they by the imposing architecture, combining an old-world grandeur with futuristic glass and gleam underneath an ostentatious centerpiece dome. The glass panes above were wired with strings of colorful lights for the nightly holiday light show. Whoop-dee-doo.

Underneath, in the large courtyard, a gigantic winter wonderland playground was set up to indoctrinate children into greed and excess at their most impressionable age. People dressed as ornaments, princesses, nutcrackers, elves, candy canes, and wrapped presents posed for pictures with children as they lined up to sit on the lap of an old fake Santa. A twenty dollar sitting fee plus another twenty-five or thirty for the picture. About the price for a lap dance at a seedy strip club.

Tyler wanted to plug his ears as he passed the line of whiny children. "I wanna," "I wanna," "I wanna."

As if the animatronics, light show, and electronic holiday music weren't enough to send a child into stimulus overload, the amount of sugar harbored by the candy canes, gingerbread snacks, and sugar cookies fueled the ferocity of temper tantrums of children being dragged away from the dazzling array of toy porn displayed prominently in the surrounding store windows.

Tyler quickened his steps and cut behind Santa's plastic throne.

"I want a papa for Christmas," a child's voice warbled from the fat man's lap.

Good luck with that, Tyler whispered under his breath. The hopeful innocence of the little girl's voice brought back his nightly prayers, kneeling at his bedside and believing God would bring his father back. Eventually his father had returned—in a body bag.

He couldn't help but peek at the source of the tiny voice. She was a sweet little girl, dressed in pink, with a mess of silver-blond curls. But what caught his eye was the woman standing behind the line, the girl's mother. She carried the air of authority and insisted her daughter meant to have a puppy. Her business-like demeanor contrasted to the fierce blush coloring her face, as if she too, had secretly wanted a man, not for a father, but for recreational purposes.

Despite her confident, upper-class aura, her clothes were ordinary: jeans, a pink sweater, and running shoes, unlike the designer outfits sported by the myriads of Christmas shoppers dripping with status symbols—diamond crusted watches and designer handbags. The woman was a looker, although not pretty in the delicate sense. Her warm brown hair was cropped in the efficient manner of a female Army officer in contrast to her elegant, fine-featured face, tiny pink lips, rosy cheeks, and a pert nose. Serious woman though. She marched her daughter away from Santa, probably upset that Jolly Ol' St. Fake had promised to grant her daughter's wish.

Didn't make sense. A woman as beautiful as she should have plenty of well-heeled men volunteering to take the position of stepfather for that sweet little girl.

A rent-a-cop tapped Tyler's shoulder. "Move along. You're not here for the Santa line, you have to stay outside the play area."

Tyler shrugged away from the guard without answering. He browsed by the Holiday Express train. Nope, he definitely wasn't interested in taking a ride. It reminded him too much of the train set his father used to set up every Christmas before he'd disappeared during the First Gulf War.

Tyler wandered toward the towering Christmas tree, craning his neck to see the star at the top. Whenever his father had been home for Christmas, Tyler had been the one who had sat on his broad shoulders and placed the star on the tip-top branch. He and his mother would have decorated the tree from the bottom up, hanging ornaments and stringing the lights, but they could never reach the top. His mother would take the golden star out of the box and place it on the mantle, waiting for the family to gather around the tree. There'd be popcorn and Christmas carols, and once his father stepped through the door, he'd pick Tyler up and hand him the star. Everyone would clap and cheer as Tyler mounted the star. It had made him feel the same as if he'd scored a game winning touchdown.

They never had another tree after his father disappeared and was later found dead.

"Mister, can you please take a picture of us?" A young woman waved her hand in front of Tyler and gestured to her group of friends.

"Sure, no problem." He took her phone. "Where's the shutter button?"

"On screen," the woman replied. "Tap the target."

"Sure." Showed how long he'd been gone. When he was deployed to Afghanistan after 9/11, the phones had push buttons and no camera feature. He shot a few poses for the family and handed the fancy contraption to the woman.

After they gathered their coats and bags from the floor, he noticed they'd left a takeout container. He picked it up and looked around, not spotting them. Not that he tried too hard. He was hungry, and the food smelled delicious. It was Chinese take out, orange chicken and chow mein. A wrapped almond cookie sat in one of the pockets of the container.

His mouth watering, Tyler swiped a fork and napkins from a nearby concession stand and sat on a bench under the massive Christmas tree. He gave thanks and dug in.

"Papa? Can I have a cookie?" a tiny voice squeaked in close vicinity. It was the little girl who'd asked for a father for Christmas.

Tyler glanced around, but didn't spot the girl's mother. "Where's your mother?"

"She's looking for you, but I found you sitting under the big Christmas tree just like Santa pwo-mised." The girl beamed expectantly at him.

"Well, it isn't Christmas yet. Still two more weeks." Tyler wiped his lips with a napkin. "Let's see if we can't find your mother."

"Okay, Papa." The girl put her hand in his. "I can't wait to tell her, Santa got you for my very own."

Tyler wanted to let her hand go. This wouldn't look good. He hastily replaced the lid on the takeout container and dangled the almond cookie. "Here, you can have the cookie, but you have to help me find your mother."

"Yay!" the little girl squealed, snatching the cookie. She ripped the wrapper and took off, running. "Mama, I found him."

Tyler pitched the rest of the food into the trash and loped after her. She could get lost in this crowd, and he wasn't sure he spotted her mother anywhere.

Sure enough, the little girl's glee turned to confusion and then fear as she whipped her head back and forth, crying, "Mama? Mama?"

The cookie dropped to the floor, and her eyes grew big. She paused to take a large breath, the kind children did right before letting out a loud scream.

Tyler reached for her hand. "Honey, don't be afraid. I'm sure your mother's looking for you."

"Mama," she yelled, screwing her fists into her eye sockets.

Several bystanders glared at him, rocking from one foot to the other, as if deciding whether to intervene or not. A woman whipped out her cell phone and snapped a picture. Great. Just great. He was about to be reported as a child kidnapper. Why couldn't he have left it to the rent-a-cops? Except who knew whether they had criminal backgrounds?

"Papa!" The girl launched herself at him, hugging him around his legs. "Mama got lost. We need to put up posters. Offer a reward."

The bystanders who had been watching Tyler smiled and shrugged with relief, apparently convinced the child was in no danger.

Tyler had no choice but to play along. The number one rule, whether in a war zone in Afghanistan or homeless in the good ol' US of A was to not draw attention. Walk as if you belonged and blend in with the background.

"Where shall we start, missy?" Tyler swung his arm alongside the girl. "What's your name, by the way?"

The girl giggled. "Didn't Mama tell you? Or Santa?"

"Uh, I must not have been paying attention."

"It's Bwee, and I'm four." She held up four fingers.

"Okay, Miss Bwee." He couldn't help smiling. "Where did you lose Mama? Was it near Santa's Throne?"

"No, Mr. Candy Man." Bwee who was probably Bree crossed her arms and tilted her jaw with a bossy pout. "I want red and green candy cane."

"So your mother was paying for the candy cane and disappeared?" Tyler led her toward the direction of the Christmas candy display. "Which one?"

"That big one, red and green. Please, Papa? Can you buy it?"

Big blue eyes peered at him as if he were a hero. How could he say no? Except for the price tag. Five dollars. Tyler dug into his pocket. He had a couple of bills from tips he collected helping elderly people carry their groceries into their apartments. Counting the change carefully, he assembled five dollars and gave it to the candy man.

Again, Bree's delighted smile wobbled his insides, reminding him of outings with his father—duck hunting, fence repairing, fishing—following his father's footsteps.

In retrospect, it had all been useless. Ten years in a war zone could not atone for his father's death or make up for the fact he'd sent him away. If he hadn't called his father a hero and looked up to him as a warrior, he would have listened to his mother and not re-enlisted.

His father's last words rang through his mind. "Son, I'm gonna make you proud of me, because I'll always be your hero."

Chapter 3

~ Kelly ~

I STARE AT THE WALL full of security monitors, praying I can spot Bree. Next to me, a team of security personnel look over the shoulder of the guy at the control panel. He flips through the camera angles, responding to commands to zoom in, turn, pan.

It's hard to see a child walking among all the adults. Would the kidnapper have changed her clothes already? Maybe put a wig on her?

I vocalize my concerns to the chief of security.

"That's a possibility," he replies. "We've set up checkpoints at all the exits. He won't get far."

"What about the one leading to the subway? There's one underground that steps directly onto the train."

"You mean BART?" the man at the console replies.

Right. BART is short for Bay Area Rapid Transit. In New York, we simply say subway or train.

"Of course that's what I mean," I snap, irritable now. "He could have taken her anywhere by now."

"True, but we're capturing every exit on the video feed." He points to a monitor showing the exit to the train station.

All I see are masses of people, some wheeling strollers and others holding children wearing winter coats.

"How can you see inside the strollers? Shouldn't you have a guard inspect every child?"

There's a loud thump as the heavy steel door opens. Two San Francisco police officers follow a security guard. They remove their caps and shake my hand, introducing themselves.

I'm questioned and repeat everything that happened starting with Bree's visit to Santa, but they want me to go further back.

"Are you involved in a custody dispute?"

"Do you have any reason to suspect someone of taking an interest in your child?"

"Have you seen any suspicious people following you around before you visited the mall?"

"Do you have enemies?"

The first three questions are a definite 'no.' Not a chance, but that last one? Who can truly know? I can't imagine my coworkers at the bank, even the interns I screwed out of a job, would waste their time trapping my child. I haven't dated since college, so there's no lurking ex-boyfriend, nor have I made any friends or enemies during my short prison stint. The girls in the cleaning crew have no idea of my past life as a banker, and no one at church envies the hard life I live.

The police tell me they've set up a press conference and ask me to rehearse what I'm going to say while I wait for the camera crew. They access my Facebook account to download pictures of Bree, and I call my mother, asking her to meet me at mall security. I'm thankful she's the calm, collected type, well, except for musical performances, but she assures me she's on her way to stand by me when I hold the press conference.

I have no clue what I'm going to say. It'll be one of those tearful appeals, the kind I always turn away from when it was someone else. I wring my hands, worrying the tissue paper into shreds, willing myself to hold it together, to concentrate on the security screens.

My eyes flash from the train to the Santa Throne to the coffee shop to the center court. A broad-shouldered man walks around the giant Christmas tree holding hands with ...

"There!" I point to the screen. "That's Bree. She's with that man."

The people in the room spring into action. They speak on walkie-talkies, lock the camera onto the man and zoom in, while others rush for the door. I scramble after them, in the wake of the two police officers.

The chief of security tries to hold me back. “Let the police handle it. It could be dangerous.”

“No way am I going to let that man hurt my daughter.” I take off running after the officers who move quickly toward the tree.

The crowds of people part when they see the officers with their hands over their holsters. My heart jumps to my throat. What if Bree’s caught in the crossfire?

“Hands up,” the police shout. “Let go of the child.”

The man slowly raises his hands. I rush toward Bree, calling her name.

A guard grabs my arm. “Stay back until they get the situation under control.”

“Bree, Mama’s here. Come here. Everything’s going to be okay.” I entreat her, but she stands still.

What’s wrong with her? She has her arms locked around the man’s legs.

He’s a large fellow, scruffy with dirty blond hair, wearing carpenter pants and a black T-shirt under a worn khaki raincoat. Typical child molester profile.

The officers move in and cuff him as I pry Bree’s arms from his legs.

He says nothing, his dark blue eyes fixed on me, as if I’m his target in all of this. Could he be a disgruntled former employee? Maybe one of the analysts I backstabbed on my way up the corporate ladder?

“That’s my papa,” Bree yells. “We was looking for you.”

“He’s her father?” the head of security says. “I thought you said there’s no custody issue.”

I stand to my full height, picking up Bree. “He’s definitely not her father. Do your job and lock him up.”

I glare at the man, noting his unkempt appearance. "You better not have hurt my daughter, or you'll have hell to pay."

"But Mama," Bree lisps, now sucking on a red and green candy cane. "Santa pwo-mised. Can we take Papa home?"

I hug and kiss Bree, shuddering at the thought of this animal hurting my precious baby. "Not right now, sweetie. Nana's waiting for us at church."

"Ma'am," the police officer says. "Are you filing charges against this man? He says he found your daughter and they were looking for you."

"Did it look like they were looking for me?" I turn Bree away from him. "He bought her a candy cane. He was obviously luring her away with him."

"Is that true?" the officer asks the man.

"I bought her the candy, but I was helping her find her mother." The man, who's still handcuffed, points his chin at me.

"Why didn't you turn her over to mall security?" the police officer asks.

"Bree wanted me to find her mother." He has the audacity to wink at me. "And I wanted to meet the lovely lady and be her hero."

"Papa!" Bree says. "Santa gave me a papa. Puhwease? Can we take him home?"

Her cuteness draws chuckles from the guards around us. A female spectator comments, "I'll take him if you don't want him."

"Am I free to leave?" the man asks the officer.

The officer turns to his partner who has the man's ID. "What do we have here?"

"Uh, name's Tyler Manning," the second officer reads from his tablet computer. "No arrest record. Army Rangers, medical discharge from service in Afghanistan."

"Tyler Manning?" My mother's voice reaches me as she grasps my arm. "Aren't you the young man who gave up football to fight the war on terror?"

Tyler nods, and a grin splits his decidedly too rugged and much too handsome face. "Yes, ma'am, that would be me."

The tide shifts among the officers and onlookers. Several bystanders snap pictures of Tyler with their camera phones.

"Are you pressing charges?" the officer says to me. "You got your daughter back."

"Only because I happened to spot him on the security camera. Otherwise, he would have gotten away with her."

"He was only trying to keep her from getting lost," a female voice cuts in. "I saw them. The little girl asked him for a cookie."

I get the distinct impression I've been outgunned by the dazzling, roguish charm of the former football player. The officers are looking at him slack-jawed and wide-eyed as if wishing they could ask for his autograph.

The tension breaks when Bree holds her arms to Mr. Manning and says, "Nana, that's my papa. See? I told you I have a real papa, not a fake one like on TV."

Everyone laughs, and the officer removes the handcuffs from Mr. Manning. The crowd of shoppers surge to the war hero, asking for his autograph or posing to take pictures with him.

One man who styles himself a reporter takes a video while saying, "A good Samaritan almost got arrested today when he helped a little girl find her mother. It turns out he's none other than Tyler Manning, former Stanford quarterback who was drafted by the Raiders before joining the Army to fight for our country."

"Let's go." I weave with Bree and my mother through the gathering crowd.

"Miss? Miss?" Another man trains his smartphone at me as if it were a microphone. "Any comments? Is Mr. Manning your daughter's father?"

"I've never seen the guy before." I sidestep the amateur reporters and head for the exit. "Mr. Manning is the last guy I want around my daughter."

He might have gotten away with attempted kidnapping due to the stupidity of hero worshippers. Arrogant jerk. Who does he think he is to flirt with me and claim Bree wanted his help so he could meet me, the so-called lovely lady?

And the way his voice caressed me, and the slow wink, as if he knew exactly who I am? Creepy. Where could I have crossed paths with him? No way are my insides jiggling with jolts of electricity because of his charmed offensive. I'm not that kind of ditz to be affected by a mere hunk of a man.

Thanks to him, I almost lost my most precious daughter. That's enough to unsettle even the iron maiden herself.

"Kelly," my mother says, taking out her car keys. "Why were you so rude to Mr. Manning? We'll never make it to church on time now."

"Mama?" Bree asks. "Is Papa coming to church?"

"He's not your father." My breath seethes through my teeth. "You're not supposed to talk to strangers."

"Do I get a time out?" She sucks on the blasted red and green jumbo candy cane. "I'm sowrry."

"Never, ever run off from me." I hug her tight. "Remember the story of the big bad wolf pretending to be grandma? That man was tricking you. You don't have a father. You have me and Nana."

Teary blue eyes blink, large like saucers. "Santa pwo-mised. He did."

Chapter 4

~ Kelly ~

"I'M IN FRONT OF YOUR apartment with the baking supplies, but I can't find a parking space." I cradle the phone between my jaw and shoulder. Mother's always doing these things to me. Last minute. Today it's picking up baking supplies for the bake sale to benefit the homeless shelter.

"Just double park," she replies. "Bree and I will come out and help."

"Stay where you are." I glance up and down the busy street. It's evening already and my cleaning shift starts in an hour. "Let me find a side street. I don't like Bree darting out into traffic."

Has Mother forgotten how unpredictable a four-year-old can be? She can sound logical and reasonable, but she's only parroting back whatever instructions I give her. Doesn't matter how many stranger danger classes I enroll her in, she's always making exceptions.

He's not a stranger. He told me his name.

I asked if she's dangerous. She says she's nice.

But he might be my father.

My stomach curdles at that last one. How can I explain to her that she truly does not have a father? After we returned from the mall, she threw a tantrum when she realized her designated father was not coming home with us.

Thankfully she'd forgotten about him the very next day, but she's back to sucking her thumb and hugging her fuzzy yellow blanket.

I'm in luck. A car pulls out of a spot a block from my mother's apartment. I flick on the signal and swoop in. Finally, something goes my way.

A block isn't too bad, except I have milk, flour, and sugar—heavy stuff. I loop a cloth tote bag over each shoulder and dangle two more bags on my forearms. Schlepping groceries is one of the things I do for my mother since she watches Bree during the evenings I work.

I make it almost a block before I hear a voice. "Need a hand, miss?"

My gaze stops at a broad chest and strong shoulders belonging to none other than Mr. Manning from the mall.

He slides a grin and tips his Giants baseball cap. "We didn't get off to a good start, I'm afraid."

"Uh, what are you doing, stalking me?" I shoot him what I hope is a killer glare.

"Actually looking to help a damsel in distress." He slides one of the bags from my arms. "Let me get those for you."

Unlike the other day at the mall, he's clean shaven and his hair's combed, although curling at the tips.

"I'm good. I can do it myself. Gimme that." I make a grab for the bag.

He dangles it out of my reach. "Only if you say you're sorry."

"Excuse me?" I sneer, almost rolling my eyes.

What planet does he live on? He tried to kidnap my daughter and got off because the police are football fans, and I owe him an apology?

"What I said." He looks in the bag. "Eggs. I love eggs."

Oh, I get it. He's panhandling. He's still wearing that ratty raincoat and a pair of grimy boots, although his jeans and flannel shirt look clean and pressed.

"Give me the bag or I'll charge you for robbery." I grit my teeth, refusing to be softened by the twinkling blue eyes and lopsided grin. He's playing a game with me, seeing how far he can push before asking for a tip.

"My, my, we're not being friendly today, are we?" He drawls and walks toward the apartment building. "Which door?"

I drop the other bags and dig for my cell phone. "I'm calling the police if you don't leave. I don't care which football team you played for or how much my mother moons about you being a hero who gave up all that money to fight the war on terror."

A cloud darkens his expression, and his eyebrows draw together. "I'm no hero and the war wasn't about terror. That's just the line they fed us sheep."

"Wh-what do you mean? You're Tyler Manning, aren't you?"

"Yeah, that's my name. And look, I'm sorry about the misunderstanding with your daughter." He puts the bag on the ground and wipes his fingers through his hair. "I meant you no harm."

Whoa. Mention of the war seems to have sobered him. The cocky grin is gone. The light-heartedness is replaced by stone, cold seriousness. The sparkle in his eyes has gone flat, and in its place is a hollow emptiness.

"Sure, none taken." I swallow as he loops the bag over my outstretched arm.

"Good evening, ma'am." He tucks his hands into his pockets, shrugs, and ambles past me toward the street corner.

"Wait, Mr. Manning," I yell out. Have I insulted him? Since meeting him, I've read every article on the internet about him. The last one was written a few months ago, one of those "whatever happened to" type articles. Apparently, he was discharged after multiple active tours and is now homeless, having given his bonus money and paychecks to Warspring International, a charity for orphans of war.

Tyler's shoulders heave, and he stops in his tracks.

I leave the bags and scramble to his side. "Look, I don't mean to be so hostile, but if you had any children, you'd understand why I have to be careful. You never know."

"I understand, ma'am. When you've seen children lose all their relatives, alone in this world, you can't help but reach out and give a hand." His mouth attempts a smile, but the lines tightened around his eyes.

Something about the sincerity of those words and the sheer sadness showing in his expression clutches my heart. I take his hand.

"You're all alone, aren't you?" My voice comes out choked. "I read about you."

"Pretty much so. Didn't have a large family when I deployed, just me and my mom, and well, the articles probably mentioned her dying a few years back, right after I reenlisted."

We stand in the lengthening shadows of the evening, our eyes locked in a silent understanding. I almost lost my mother to cancer. During her entire treatment plan, I only took a few days off from my relentless banking schedule. I was given a second chance. Tyler wasn't as fortunate.

His hand is strong and warm, solid, protective. I can see why Bree trusts him—a man like him, a trained killer, yet, gentle with the weak and most helpless.

He gives my fingers a caressing squeeze and darts his eyes at my bags of groceries sprawled on the sidewalk. "I can help you take those up, but if you'd rather not let me know where you live, that's okay too. You better get the milk and eggs into the refrigerator."

"Yeah, I better go." I dig into my purse for my wallet and extract a five. "Here."

He raises both hands and backs away. "Not asking for a handout, ma'am."

"Kelly, call me Kelly. I thought I could help. Or at least pay you back for the candy cane."

"That's my Christmas gift to Bree. Bye." He waves and strides off, cutting between two cars and into the street.

"Mama!" Bree's voice calls from the building entrance. "Nana say we help with gwo-ce-wies."

Did she see Tyler? I glance over my shoulder, but he's gone already.

~ Tyler ~

Tyler peered at Kelly, her mother, and Bree from behind the bus stop barrier. They belonged together, had each other: grandmother, mother, daughter.

Was there no man in their lives? What kind of guy would abandon little Bree, a sweet child, so trusting and innocent? He had to be a real chump, an idiot. The thought that he'd had Kelly in his arms, impregnated her, and left her, had Tyler raging at the unknown douchebag. These civilians never appreciated what they had, took family for granted. Left women to fend for themselves with their children. He hadn't gone to Afghanistan to fight for a delinquent father. He'd fought and sacrificed so women like Kelly would have a better life, a chance to live free from terror, or so he'd been told.

What he wouldn't give to be the man who'd fathered Bree. If only he could be the guy they'd look up to, he'd protect and cherish them, never let them fear anyone or anything.

But it was too late now. He'd been damaged by the war, a mental case. Despite the media coverage after the mall incident depicting him as a war hero, a humanitarian soldier, he was in reality a homeless bum, a nobody.

His gaze lingered at the gate where Kelly's fluid figure had disappeared into the courtyard. For a moment, she'd made him feel like a man, a healthy blush coloring her delicate complexion, her honey-brown hair fluttering in the wind—right before she offered him money.

He crushed his fingers around the coins in his pocket. He was no charity case. He didn't need a roof over his head, especially in a mild climate like San Francisco. Ten years in Afghanistan with extreme temperatures ranging from blistering hot summers with moisture sucking sandstorms to bone-jarring winter freezes taught him to appreciate the temperate, coastal luxury of California.

If you had children, you'd understand. Kelly's words echoed in his mind. Even without children of his own, he more than understood. Thousands and thousands of hungry eyes, gaping mouths, dried tears on dirt streaked faces, empty hands, bloated bellies of malnutrition. He didn't need a house. They needed every penny of his benefits check.

Tyler jogged down the staircase to the underground BART station to pick up tips. People arriving from the airport needed his help, as did mothers toting children and groceries.

"Hey, hey, War Hero!" The smooth, musical voice of his buddy, Sawyer, vibrated in the tunnel. "Saw you on the news. That really your kid?"

Tyler clapped Sawyer on the shoulder and bumped his fist. "In another life. How's busking today?"

Sawyer patted his acoustic guitar. "Made me a pile singing Christmas carols."

"With your voice? Bet they're paying you to shut up."

"Heck, you ought to get a gig going with me. You sing and strut, the chicks go nuts over you, and I collect the tips."

Tyler waved his friend off. "The only thing important to me are the checks going to the children."

Sawyer strummed a minor blues chord on his guitar and swung around to block him. "Get over it, bud. What happened happened. Your suffering isn't going to bring any of them back."

"Shut it." Tyler shoved his friend. He didn't need anyone analyzing him. He wasn't suffering. He was alive, living in San Francisco with two hands, arms, legs, and feet. A whole man able to work and help others. He crossed to the platform where the lights flashed announcing the arrival of a train in five minutes.

The rumbling in the tunnel blends with the footsteps pounding behind me. A thunderous roar detonates, and the clatter of machine gun fire rattles up above. The flashes from their muzzles burst jagged like lightning. Bullets chew up the concrete, and heat tears through the shrapnel scarred station.

I duck and roll, grabbing for my M4. Where is it? My head's bare, and I've lost my helmet and flak jacket. Fire streaks overhead. I grab for a grenade, anything to lob back at them. Shrieks of metal grinding against metal scream through my head. I take a defensive position behind a pillar, my breath ragged. Where are my guys? I can't abandon them. I must be the decoy. Draw the fire so they can live. My legs shaking like rubber, I charge the machine gun nest.

Grenades explode all around me, tearing holes and cracking the concrete. One lands next to me, unexploded. I lob it back at the shooters. A metallic rattle echoes behind me. What is it? I unsheathe my K-Bar knife and slash. The enemies scream, hollering. A grenade punches me in the gut, detonating in my face.

My nerves scream, sizzle and zap. Electric sparks and arcs stop my heart. I lose control of my arms, legs, voice. The smell of cordite and blood overcomes me. Am I dead? Where's Mother? Dad? A white light blinds me and I feel nothing.

Chapter 5

~ Kelly ~

"LOOKS LIKE YOUR MR. MANNING caused quite a commotion at the BART station." Mom yawns and thumps her mug of hot chocolate.

I'm tired and achy after my cleaning shift at the Mogul Bank building. Leaning over, I kiss my mother's temple.

"Thanks for watching Bree. She asleep?"

"Yeah," Mom says, more interested in the TV. "I don't think they'll show it again. Maybe they have it on the internet."

I stretch my arms and yawn, trying really hard not to be annoyed. "He's not my Mr. Manning, and he can shoot up the BART station for all I care."

So not true. Jitters of anxiety rocket in my gut, and I wonder what happened to Tyler. When I get home, I'll look over the local news sites. I can't show any interest in a man without Mom practically pushing me into his arms, as if all I need to solve my problems is a man. She never understood why I chose to have Bree by myself, why I never wanted to marry. She thinks I'm a control freak, that I want everything done my way. I choose to view it differently. I'm efficient, organized, even ruthless in business. What need do I have for a ball and chain called a man when a piece of plastic with long life batteries does a much better job?

I open the refrigerator and pour myself a glass of almond milk. Mom's still clicking, her eyes intent on the laptop screen.

I drain the almond milk and rinse out the glass, then step toward the bedroom. Bree's face is pale in the moonlight streaming through the window. Her thumb is stuck in her mouth. I remove it with a pop, and she grimaces, her face twisted as if someone stole a lollipop from her.

I wrap the blanket around her, taking care not to wake her. I can't help but kiss her, run my fingers through the fine, silky hair. She smells pure and clean, like soap and powder. Times like this make it all worthwhile. I'd do anything for Bree, just like I risked it all for Mom.

Bree stirs in my arms, mumbling, "Will you be my Daddy?"

I rock her, and her thumb goes back into her mouth. I thought she was over her father obsession after the tantrum. She seemed satisfied with my explanation of different families. Some have two mothers, others have two fathers, or a single mother, a lone dad, but the best ones have a grandmother. Sure. I hate my lies, but honestly, she was happy enough before I went to jail.

Hefting her over my shoulder, I sweep by the kitchen. Mom looks over and starts to say something, but I put my finger over my lips.

She loops a plastic bag over my wrist. "A sample of the cookies Bree and I made."

Bree sleeps the entire way to my apartment, a cheap ground floor unit south of Golden Gate Park. It's actually carved out of someone's house, walled off with a single bathroom and kitchenette with a separate entrance through a sliding glass door. Nothing in San Francisco is truly affordable, but the cleaners at Mogul Bank are paid higher wages than most, and for some perverse reason, I feel at home among the investment bankers working twenty-four by seven in the building. Even the year round freezing temperature of the air conditioning and the bright lights in the middle of the night keep the blood humming through my veins. Just overhearing the conversations and feeling the high stress levels invigorate me. My probation officer assures me I can be of use in their investigations against insider trading, infiltrate a bank and catch crooks for the government, but right now, I just want to lie low and not let anyone know who I used to be.

After tucking Bree into her bed, I boot up my laptop and scan the local news for Tyler Manning.

A headline reads, "PTSD episode hospitalizes former Stanford quarterback."

Below it are pictures of Tyler, the one on the left showing him in his football uniform while the one on the right is a mug shot, his eyes glazed as if watching an endless horror flick.

Witnesses say Tyler freaked out when the train approached the platform. He ran around shouting and pantomiming shooting, grenade throwing and knifing, until he was shocked by a stun gun wielded by another homeless veteran.

"I got to him before the transit police. He's not violent," the veteran said in a video interview. "But the police might have shot him dead. This isn't the first time he had a lucid flashback."

I don't know why I should care. Tyler Manning's obviously another wounded warrior, a shell-shocked guy having difficulties adjusting to civilian life. He could be dangerous, or so I tell myself. Definitely not the type of man I want anywhere near me and my family, especially Bree.

My eyes dart between his two pictures, the young, brash, confident quarterback, a scholar-athlete in contrast to the broken, haunted veteran wandering the streets without a home, without family or anyone to care for him.

Alone.

~ Tyler ~

Tyler mulled over the prescriptions. Anti-depressants, anti-anxiety, treatments for bipolar disorder.

"Make sure you take as directed and don't stop or skip a dose," the psychiatrist said. "I also want you to sign up for therapy."

"May I go now?" Tyler rubbed the back of his neck. The night spent on the hospital bed was restful, but he didn't deserve to be comfortable.

"Not until after this afternoon's therapy session." The psychiatrist tapped notes into his electronic tablet. "The nurse will give you your first dose."

Tyler hated taking drugs. Heck, he'd never even smoked pot. Being out of control or under the influence wasn't safe. His buddies had always riled on him for being boring, a hypervigilant stick in the mud, always prepared, but apparently not enough to save them from a child strapped with bombs.

The nurse counted the tablets and handed Tyler a cup of water. If he wanted to get out of here, he'd have to convince the doctors of his compliance, so he swallowed the cocktail of pills.

"Thank you, ma'am." He tipped the glass of water back and drank.

"Great," she said, a saccharine smile plastered on her face. "Now I can let your visitor in."

Visitor? Why would Sawyer lose precious hours busking and visit him in this depressing place? The gray walls were enough gloom to drive the laughter out of a troop of clowns—not that clowns had anything to laugh about when everyone was laughing at them.

Tyler pinned his gaze to the doorway, his ears pricked as footsteps approached.

"Are you a relative?" the nurse asked.

"Friend." Kelly stood at the doorway. Her hair was soft around her face, and she wore a turquoise stretch shirt and white jeans.

"Friend?" he muttered, unable to keep from staring at her.

"I thought you could use some company." She set a pink plastic container on the bed tray. "Cookies. My mother and Bree made them."

Tyler's throat froze, and he had to consciously close his mouth so he wouldn't look like a gaping idiot. "Th-thanks for coming. I don't know what to say."

"My pleasure." Kelly opened the box. "Christmas cookies. Have one?"

"Uh, sure." Tyler blinked to reassure himself she was truly there. He picked a lopsided green tree cookie with red and white sprinkles. "Thanks."

"May I sit?" Kelly gestured to the chair at the side of the bed.

"Be my guest." The cookie was sweet in his mouth, buttery and fragrant with vanilla. Frosted and sprinkled by Bree's little fingers.

Kelly propped herself on the side of the chair, sitting ramrod straight and smoothed her hair. "How are you feeling?"

"Okay." He hated the sympathetic look on her face. He didn't need her pity, and he shouldn't be in this hospital bed. There wasn't anything wrong with him. He set the half-uneaten cookie on the tray. "Thanks for dropping by. I need to get going."

Her gaze swept over the bare room, taking in the fact he had no silverware, no lines, or cords, not even sheets thin enough to make a noose. All that was missing were the padded walls.

"Are you telling me to leave?"

"No, ma'am. I'm not up for visiting. I have work to do. Places to go."

"Indeed." Her chin tilted up so she was looking down her nose at him. "You're trying to get rid of me."

"No, ma'am. I appreciate you coming, but I'm really okay. There's nothing wrong with me."

"Call me Kelly." She crossed her arms. "I didn't say there's anything wrong with you. I thought you needed a friend, but if you don't, I have lots to do."

He couldn't help narrowing his eyes. If she thought she was doing her good deed of the day, then she should visit someone at the children's hospital, not a maniacal veteran subject to panic attacks. Besides, this was the worst place he wanted her to see him—sitting on a bed in the psych ward, drugged, and wearing a flimsy gown.

"I appreciate you coming," Tyler said. "I'm just surprised."

"Why? Because you think I'm an ice queen?" Her gaze wandered over his torso, and she lifted a finger, almost touching the tail end of the mythical sea serpent tattoo winding around his arm.

His muscles tightened and twitched, the air electrifying between them. The last woman who'd ran her fingers over his ink was his mother from her deathbed. He'd sat at her side, explaining the symbolism and meaning, stories he made up on the spot—an old mariner on a persistent search for phantom love, always behind the next wave, never to be attained.

"I'm thinking you're anything but icy." He cleared his throat, but his voice was too husky, thick. "I could use a friend. Thanks."

The color rose in her cheeks, and she blinked. "I never thanked you for finding Bree, and I was rude to you yesterday, offering you money. Forgive me?"

"There's nothing to forgive." Tyler forced his attention to the sugar cookies. Her conciliatory mood brought blood surging through his veins, but he had to maintain control. "Especially when you come bearing Christmas gifts."

A smile played on her face, brightening her greenish-brown eyes. "We're having a toy drive at our church this Saturday and need people to wrap the gifts. There's a meal for all the volunteers and, well, if you're not doing anything ..."

Warmth spread over Tyler's chest and his heartbeat quickened. Was she asking him on a date? Or was it simply a mission of mercy? Making sure he had a hot meal? Whichever, she'd cared enough about him to visit and invite him to church. Maybe she was receptive to him being more than friends.

"Sounds great," he replied. "But I'd rather take you to dinner afterwards. What's your favorite food?"

"Oh, I couldn't do that to you." She wiped her hands on her jeans. "Living out on the streets is hard enough."

"Kelly." He took her hand and pressed it. "What's hard is not having a friend. Someone to talk to."

"I know, Mr. Manning. But I'd like to limit our interaction to the church. I don't really know you, and I have a daughter to protect. I'm already taking a chance to come see you, but I wanted to help."

Shot down. She saw him as a charity case, a chance to do good and ease her conscience on having been rude to him—a troubled homeless war veteran in need of Christ and a hot meal.

Tyler dropped Kelly's hand. "I'm doing fine without you, ma'am. I'm glad I helped Bree, and honestly, I'm not interested in being her father or stalking you or getting a handout from your church. Whatever you think you need me to forgive is forgiven. Whiteboard's clean."

Chapter 6

~ Kelly ~

"TYLER MANNING ASKED YOU ON a date and you turned him down?" My younger sister, Ella, creases the wrapping paper while I tape the ends. "Unbelievable."

"He wanted to feed me. I wouldn't call that a date." I scan the tables of volunteers in case he decided to show up. Not that he even knows where our church is, since I didn't bother to leave him a printed tract with directions.

"But Mom says he asked you to dinner."

I don't know why I blab so much to Mom. Well, I was thrilled, even though I turned him down. Tyler Manning's a prime catch no matter what, but I have Bree to think about. Dating Tyler would get her hopes up, what with her obsession on finding a father.

I tape a bow to the wrapped toy and pick up a boxed game. "He only asked because he has too much pride. I told him we have a hot meal for the volunteers, and he took it wrong."

Ella flicks her fingers through her spiky blond hair and elbows her boyfriend Jaden. "You believe her? She's so independent, doesn't need a man. She does everything herself. She can't even let a guy pay for her dinner."

"You blew it, Kelly," Jaden says. "It would have been so cool to have Tyler Manning here wrapping gifts. Think of the publicity, the camera crews, and the money we could raise for the women and children's shelter."

"That's the problem." I thump the game on the table and unroll a sheet of wrapping paper. "No one cares how Tyler really feels. Everyone wants a story, a publicity stunt, a piece of him. You should have seen the stories they wrote about his nervous breakdown."

Ever since news got out that I visited Tyler at the Veteran's Hospital, reporters have been hounding me, asking whether I would allow Mr. Manning to play at being Bree's father, whether he had any plans on getting back to football, whether the charity he supports would take him on as a spokesman.

"I understand." Ella shoots Jaden a pointed look. "The man suffers from post traumatic stress. He doesn't need all this publicity. Must be sad when you think how awesome he used to be, a football star, and everything he gave up for that stupid war."

"From hero to big fat zero." A deep voice drawls behind us.

"Tyler!" I gulp, almost choking. "You came. How'd you find us?"

He tips his Giants baseball cap. "I'm a stalker, remember?"

That grin of his trips my heartbeat, and I wish I could throw my arms around him. Meanwhile, my stomach cringes, and I wonder how much he heard.

Jaden and Ella must be worried too because they're suddenly busy curling ribbons and darting nervous glances at Tyler.

I take his elbow and turn him toward them. "Tyler, this is my sister, Ella, and her boyfriend, Jaden."

Ella reaches out to shake his hand. "I heard you're Bree's hero. Thanks for finding her."

Jaden bumps fists with Tyler. "I saw you play for Stanford."

Tyler points both index fingers at him. "You must have been what, five years old?"

"Ten. My sister had such a crush on you. Did you know her? Melisa Sloup? Class of 2004?"

"Melisa, Melisa, of course." Tyler laughs, his face visibly relaxing, and he winks. "I might have had a crush on her too."

For a moment there, he looks like the golden boy again. The curly tips of blond hair gleam under his baseball cap, and laugh lines crinkle around his eyes. My jealous heart thuds at his fond remembrance of Jaden's sister. How many women must he have had? Star athlete, handsome as Hollywood, and charming. Way out of my league. I'd been the queen of nerds, nose in a book, weekends and evenings spent with financial formulas and spreadsheets instead of parties and boys.

The rest of the volunteers gather around, recognizing Tyler's celebrity. My mother's missing all this, since she's home with Bree. I can't believe people are having their pictures taken with him. Single women swarm him, welcoming him to our church. They're sizing him up, ticking off pluses and minuses, wondering if he's a Christian, whether he'll find a job or lead a youth group.

"Ella, get over here. We're not going to have the presents wrapped before the ladies bring in dinner." I yank my sister's sleeve to remove her from the gawking females. Not that Jaden seems to mind. He's busy snapping pictures.

"What about them?" Ella gestures to the giggling, squealing women. "You have first dibs on him. Why aren't you staking your claim?"

"He's a homeless vet, and he has issues. They're wasting their time." I huff and cut through a swath of wrapping paper.

"Ah, but each of them thinks they can fix him better than the other, and I'd say he's worth it. They don't make them more manly than Tyler Manning."

~ Tyler ~

The presents were wrapped, and the buffet table was piled high with casseroles, noodle dishes, Filipino egg rolls or *lumpia*, and even a whole roast suckling pig, or as the excited women called it, *lechón*.

Tyler was surprised at the diversity of Pacific Baptist Church. It seemed in the ten years since he'd been gone that the Bay Area had become truly international. Beautiful women from the Philippines, Ecuador, Puerto Rico, Haiti, and Costa Rica swarmed around him, each offering up dishes from their home country.

He'd never had Filipino spaghetti before, sweet with sliced hotdogs. The woman who made it, Francine, even put pepperoni in hers and laced it with cheddar cheese.

Meanwhile, Davina from Puerto Rico wanted him to try the *pasteles*, a tamale made of plantains with meats and spices wrapped in parchment paper.

He was plied with *tres leches*, a sponge cake soaked with three types of milk, sweet potato pudding pie, peppermint bark, and hot cider eggnog.

A missionary gave a presentation on Christmas in the Solomon Islands, and one of his daughters showed Tyler her pet bird, a bright green Solomon Island eclectus parrot who said, "Believe."

Tyler hadn't felt as carefree and alive for a long time, but the lights were too bright and the women's voices too high-pitched. His senses were on full alert, and he startled when someone dropped a stack of plates, his hand automatically going to where the pistol grip of his M4 would be. He breathed in slowly through his nose, inhaling the fragrant scents, the aromas of the food, the smell of gunpowder. No. Not gunpowder. Wax candles and paraffin warming trays.

The hubbub of voices around him pounded in his ear, although softer than the booming of mortar shells. He looked for Kelly, but she had disappeared into the kitchen.

She'd avoided him all evening, sat at a table far from him after manning the buffet line, carving and serving the suckling pig. Throughout dinner, she'd kept her gaze averted from him and hustled around serving dessert, cleaning messes, and pouring coffee and tea. If her purpose for inviting him was to give him a square meal, she'd succeeded.

"Have another slice of pie?" a pretty Asian lady said.

Tyler rubbed his belly and shook his head. "I'm going to explode."

"Will you come back for the Christmas pageant next week? How about Wednesday evening? We have choir practice and we'll go caroling at Union Square the entire week before Christmas."

"Sounds interesting, thanks." Tyler gave her a smile and checked his watch. The weather had turned cold and drizzly, and he wasn't looking forward to his spot under a highway bridge. If he wanted a bed at the shelter, he'd better get going.

"Papa!" Bree skipped toward him, her arms stretched wide. "Santa told me you're an elf. A big elf, like that green one on TV."

Her grandmother clapped a hand over the child's mouth. "You can't go around calling him 'Papa.'"

Tyler laughed and patted Bree on the head. "How about you call me Ty? That's my big elf name."

"Like tying my shoes?" Bree lisped. "I know how to tie my own shoes."

"Wow, you have to show me," Tyler said.

Bree plopped herself on the floor and untied her tennis shoes. "They show me at pwee-school. I'm a big girl."

She looped the knot around her finger and retied her shoes.

Tyler clapped. "Now, you remember my name, Ty, just like your shoes."

"Yay! But I wish you my papa." Bree's thumb went into her mouth.

Out of the side of his eye, Tyler saw the group of single women whispering and pointing to Bree. Oh well, he didn't mind her messing up his reputation. He wasn't in any position to date or flirt with any of them. No woman really understood what he wanted from life. To them, it was all about snagging a husband with a stable paycheck and making him fit into the mortgage, child-rearing, college tuition paying schedule.

"Where's your mother?" Tyler asked Bree.

Kelly's mother scanned the room. "Kelly's around here somewhere. Probably in the kitchen cleaning up. Why don't I find her for you?"

"No, don't bother on my account." Tyler stood and stretched. "I have to line up at the shelter if I want a bed. Looks like a storm coming in."

"Oh my. You're right," Kelly's mother said. "It's going to be howling out there. Windy and raining. You must stay with me. I have an extra bedroom."

"Thanks, ma'am, but I can't." Tyler pulled his raincoat from the folding chair. "It wouldn't be right."

"Call me Peggy, and I won't take no for an answer."

"Please, please?" Bree said, her hands clasped in a praying position. "God says to be nice for Christmas. You can stay and play with me."

"Uh, I'm not sure your mother would like that." Tyler backed toward the door. "I better get going. The meal was delicious, and I'm stuffed."

"Tyler Manning." Kelly's mother, Peggy, put her hands on her hips. "I have a light bulb I need changing, and it's too high for me to reach. I also have to change the batteries for my smoke detectors. Think you can give me a hand?"

"I can do that for you tomorrow." He tipped his baseball cap at her. "But, I must be going. Thanks."

"Then you'll stay for dinner tomorrow evening. Promise me," Peggy said. "I'll have a nice roast in the oven, sweet potatoes on the side, and green bean casserole."

"Cookies, too." Bree clapped her hands. "I lick the fwosting and spwinkles."

He glanced around for Kelly, but she was nowhere in sight.

Peggy had a right to make friends whether Kelly approved or not. Besides, he wasn't done with Kelly, not by a long shot. If she thought she could brush him off as a charity case, she was mistaken. Behind that self-reliant exterior was a woman, a strong one, but one who had needs. And judging by her incessant blushing, she probably hadn't had a man since the night she conceived Bree.

Reaching over to shake Peggy's hand, Tyler straightened his back and stood to his full height. "Looking forward to it, ma'am, er, Peggy. Make a list of everything you need done, and I'll see you tomorrow."

Chapter 7

~ Kelly ~

"I CAN'T BELIEVE YOU INVITED Tyler to your apartment." I close my eyes and shake my head at my mother, my hand over my forehead. "How do you know he's not dangerous? What were you thinking offering him the room where Bree stays?"

"It was close to freezing last night, and with the wind and rain, I didn't want him to catch a cold." Mom draws the curtains back. "Look out there."

It's morning, but the storm hasn't relented. Tree branches dance in the howling wind, and rainwater sloshes against the windows. No one should have been outdoors last night.

My chest hollows and my stomach contracts. "Do you think Tyler got a bed? The shelters are overcrowded and turn away able-bodied men."

"Then I should have insisted." Mom purses her lips and huffs. "The man is too polite and scared of you. I can tell. He looked around for you when I asked him to come over."

"Me? He's the one surrounded by all the single women at the church."

"Can we admit you're officially jealous?" Mom chuckles. "I saw you glaring at the women talking to him."

"I was only pissed they weren't doing any of the work. I could care less if they flirt with him." I pour cereal for Bree. "When's he coming over? I don't want you and Bree to be alone with him."

The bell rings. Speak of the devil. I march to the door and peek through the peephole. Sure enough, it's Tyler.

I open the door. His eyes seem to light up when he spots me, and a grin brightens his face. He's carrying a plastic toolbox.

"Thanks for inviting me to your church." He shakes the water from his raincoat.

"Did you get enough to eat?"

"Gosh, that was the best meal I had in a long time." He rubs his stomach. Well, in his case, it's likely to be a six-pack slab of muscle. "I owe you dinner."

"You don't give up, do you?" Something sinful tingles low in my gut. It can't be his sparkling god-like looks or the whiff of sporty cologne over his well-muscled chest. It has to be indigestion or something I ate last night. "Well, come in. My mother's expecting you."

"Mannings don't give up." He steps into the apartment. "When are you free?"

"I have work today, and my mother already invited you to dinner, so I'll see you this evening." I back into the kitchen and kiss Bree on the top of her head.

Today, I'm going to do the year-end books for her preschool. Since they're closed for the holidays, I'll have time to work with the owner on last minute deductions and expenses in preparation for tax season.

Tyler sets his toolbox on the floor and greets my mother with a kiss on the cheek. Since when have they gotten so close? I swear this is a conspiracy.

Bree jumps from her chair and reaches for a hug, and when he picks her up, swinging her around, I gulp as my heart contracts. Her blond hair and blue eyes make her look more like his daughter than mine.

I grab my briefcase. I don't think I can stomach the three of them, looking like they're in for a day of family fun while I have to go to work.

"Bye, Mom, Bree," I yell as I exit the apartment.

"Bye," they reply, but half-heartedly, their attention focused on Tyler's jokes.

I turn the corner where the mailboxes are set. Footsteps sound behind me.

"Kelly."

It's Tyler. He jogs up to me. "If you're worried about me being around Bree without you, I'll come back another day. I saw your expression when you were leaving, and I don't want to cause you any pain."

"You'd do that?"

"Yes, I'm the outsider here, and I can't blame you for being careful." He takes my hand and rubs it. "How about you get to know me first without them around? Then if you don't think I'm suitable, I'll leave all of you alone."

His expression is solemn, and I can't help but be drawn in by his sincerity. And face it, he's hot, rugged, tanned and very male. My hormones race, and my heart rate elevates. Those strong arms and shoulders beckon me to tuck myself into them, seek shelter and protection, not that I need them. I can stand on my own.

But a little voice nags, *Isn't it better to stand together with someone than on your own?*

Not if he hems me in. Takes away my freedom.

I swallow a mixture of drool and a lump. "How do you propose I get to know you? Shall I interview you? Check your references?"

He lifts my hand to his lips and kisses it, long and soft. "Let me buy you dinner. Take you on a date. Wherever you want."

Swoon. At least if I were the swooning type, I'd be on the floor already in a puddle. The tingly shots traveling from my hand to my toes weaken my knees and turn my belly to mush. I must resist, at least not let him know what effect he has on me.

"I'm busy right now. Working, but later this afternoon, I have some Christmas shopping to do since I was interrupted the last time I went to the mall when Bree disappeared."

"If the weather clears, let's meet under the clock outside the San Francisco Ferry Building."

"There aren't any toy stores there," I protest. See what I mean? He's already dictating the agenda to me.

"It's not far from the Exploratorium and there'll be street vendors this time of the year. I'm sure we'll find Bree something educational and fun."

"I don't know." I draw my hand from his and head toward the stairs. "I better get to work."

"Sure, where would you like to go?" His strides keep up with mine easily.

What the heck. His idea's as good as mine. I can afford to let him take the lead. It's not as if I'm going to be dating him long term.

"Ferry Building it is. See you around one. Unless it's still raining."

~ *Tyler* ~

"Yes!" Tyler jogged around the corner from Peggy's apartment complex toward the shed where he stored his clothes. "Please, God, take the rain away."

This was important. He had a date with Kelly. She was warming to him, proving he hadn't totally lost his touch with women.

By the time he walked several blocks, the rain had slackened and the sun peeked through the clouds. *Thank you, God.*

"What are you so bright-eyed and bushy-tailed about?" his friend Sawyer greeted him.

Tyler unlocked the shed he rented in the yard of a transmission shop where Sawyer worked. "Kelly agreed to go shopping with me this afternoon."

"A date? Woohoo. When was the last time you had sex?"

"Excuse me? It's shopping, not sex." Tyler picked out his only pair of black jeans. He hadn't met a woman who challenged him since Melisa back at Stanford. Ever since he returned from his tour of duty, women hadn't been high on his list of things to deal with. But Kelly? She was interesting and beautiful in a shy sort of way. Little by little, she was coming out of her shell. For him.

Sawyer threw his head back and laughed. "Didn't you know shopping leads to sex? It all depends on what you buy her. Flowers, chocolates, maybe a bottle of wine. You need any money?"

Tyler fingered the wad of bills in his pocket, an advance on the handyman work Peggy gave him. "Nah, I'm good. Got a job."

"A real one? Cool."

"Temporary handyman."

Sawyer flexed his fingers. "I'm sure you're real handy."

Shaking his head, Tyler punched Sawyer's upper arm. "Rein in your imagination. Kelly's not the type of woman to succumb to my charms."

"Then you gotta up your game, man." Sawyer took a beaded stone necklace from his neck and placed it around Tyler's. "An Energy Muse Performance Necklace, bloodstone, black onyx, tiger's eye, rutilated quartz and an ancient Chinese coin for good fortune."

"Thanks, man. I'm going to hit the showers at the Y and catch you later."

"I want the complete scoop." Sawyer gave him a thumbs up. "Performance, man. Endurance. Think, 'I am an unlimited being.'"

Chapter 8

~ Kelly ~

I GASP WHEN I SPY Tyler standing under the arch of the clock tower. He hasn't spotted me yet, so I have a chance to check him out long and slow. The wind and rain from the night before had died down, and the weather's on the cool side, but not freezing.

He's wearing a black leather bomber jacket, and his legs are encased in thin black jeans over black boots. The warm blue chambray shirt is open at the collar, and a beaded necklace with an antique Chinese coin hangs around his neck. His hair is trimmed shorter on the sides, but full and wavy on top, and he's clean shaven.

If you ask me, he doesn't look like he's homeless. Could he be pretending for publicity's sake? *Homeless veteran donates entire benefit check to war orphan's charity.*

If so, that would make him a poseur and a phony. I pat down my hair. I'm only meeting him for shopping, not a date, even though I took care to apply lipstick and eyeliner and changed into a bold geometric print handkerchief hemmed dress.

Tyler turns as I draw near, and the way his eyebrows rise when he spies me sends a sizzle of excitement up my spine. It's the recognition of attraction, the scent of desire, the activation of the primitive mating urge.

His gaze dances over the interlocked diagonal Navajo patterns of my dress. Simmering warmth invades my belly, and I loop my hand around the elbow he offers.

"Hungry?" he asks. "There are quite a few gourmet shops in there with tasty snacks, organic and fair-trade."

Try expensive. I'm not about to spend the meager amount I saved for Bree, Mom, and Ella's Christmas gifts on oak-aged balsamic vinegar or smoked chili chocolate truffles. But we're here, and it'll be fun to enjoy the sights and smells and pretend to be gourmands.

Tyler leads me through the arched entrance into a tunnel-like steel structure. The ceilings soar high and open with skylights over the bustle and noise of the holiday crowd. A dazzling array of sights and heavenly scents emanate from the storefronts. Long lines queued for basic necessities like coffee and bread.

"Isn't this place amazing?" Tyler asks, leaning close to speak in my ear. "What would you like? There are raw oysters, artisan breads, truffles."

"Let's see if there are any samples." I squeeze into the olive oil shop where they have bits of bread crust for dipping and tasting.

"Hey, don't worry about sampling," Tyler says. "I've a bit of money and want to buy you something you've never tried before."

Truthfully, there's not much I hadn't enjoyed when I was an investment banker where we drank thousand dollar brandies and laced our bread crusts with caviar. But Tyler doesn't know this, and I'd rather keep it this way.

"You don't have to," I reply. "Let's walk around and enjoy the sights. We can play a game. You point to something, and I'll guess whether you'd like it or not."

We wander from the organic honey display to the stalls selling goat cheese, marvel at the variety of rustic breads and rolls, and sample bourbon-bacon jam on apple biscuits. I've seen it all before, and whatever Tyler points to, I've a reasonable shot of guessing what a guy from middle America would try, mainly comfortable, American staples like plain biscuits and milk chocolate, hot dog rolls and bland cheese.

"How'd you know I wouldn't like the Swiss chard blend with Andalusian goat cheese, lobster mushrooms, pine nuts and raisins?" He sticks his tongue out and hands me the empanada he sampled.

I pop it into my mouth. "Mmm ... You need to broaden your horizons."

"Ha, try sitting in a desert chowing down on MREs, packaged army rations, for ten years."

"I've heard Afghan food is quite delectable. The spices are fragrant, and the cooking method is healthy."

"Never had a chance to mingle with the natives."

"Then you must go with me to Little Kabul. The kebobs are to die for." Oops. Did I just say 'to die?'

"I'm not sure I ever want to go back to anywhere named Kabul." He exits with me from the empanada shop. "I'm quite satisfied to be back in the good ol' USA."

Me? The more hyphenated foreign place names, the better. The only thing I regret about my new, downsized lifestyle is the inability to travel. Someday, I'll get back into financing and give Bree the opportunity to study abroad and visit all the wonders of the world.

Tyler takes me past a store selling macarons, petite sandwich-like pastries in a plethora of delightful colors and flavors. I pick the mango hot curry, and he gets the plain vanilla. Figures.

"I'm curious about you," he says. "You seem to be quite at home among this crowd of well-heeled yuppies."

"I doubt they'd like to be called yuppies." I laugh. "Hipsters, progressives, trend setters, but definitely not yuppie."

"Oh, excuse me," he says, munching on the tiny meringue cookie with the buttercream filling. "Last I checked when I deployed, it was yuppies."

"We haven't had yuppies since the eighties. I bet that was back before you were born."

He quirks his eyebrow. "You're trying to find out when I was born."

"I already know. 1982." I stuff the rest of the crisp, spicy cookie into my mouth. "Same as me."

"Perfect."

I wonder what he means by that. We're the same age. So? The macarons go too fast. They're really tiny and expensive. Tyler asks me what my mother and Bree's favorite flavors are and gets back in line to buy a gift box. I wonder where he's getting all the money.

He shows me the tiny box. "I bought Bree a candy-cane flavor and your mother the double toffee chocolate. There's a surprise for you too."

"You didn't have to." I hesitate before remembering my manners. "Thank you. It was sweet of you." *And spendy too.*

"It's Christmas." He takes my hand, and we walk out of the shop. "How was work this morning? You don't have Christmas break?"

"Not in my line of work."

"How so?" His tone is casual, but I can tell he's curious. Part of me doesn't want to admit I'm in a cleaning service. I mean, I did work in financial services, and this morning I was working the books for the preschool.

"Year end tax planning. We have to make sure we understand the tax situation before the end of the year and make adjustments, take last minute deductions, that kind of thing."

"You're an accountant?"

"Part time and volunteer. That was Bree's preschool I help out with. In exchange, they lower her tuition."

"What do you do at nights? Your mother says you leave Bree with her every evening."

I let go of his hand and stop in the middle of a courtyard in front of the statue of Gandhi. I notice he's missing his glasses again. Vandals break them off as fast as the city can replace them. I take a deep breath, wondering why my mother's so open with him.

"I'm sorry, I didn't mean to pry," Tyler says, as he leans against the concrete base of the statue.

"It's okay, we're trying to get to know each other, so it's a fair question. The truth is I have a degree in finance from Princeton, but I'm now working as a custodian."

"You gotta do what you gotta do." He puts his arm around me. "Lots of people were downsized."

"Yeah, true." I shrink under his scrutiny. "You know what? I'm thirsty. Shall we get something to drink?"

"Good idea." He scans the sign boards advertising organic smoothies. "I could get you one of those gluten-free, kale, avocado, chia seed concoctions."

"No way. Hot apple cider toddy with a shot of Jack Daniels for me." We weave through the crowds back to one of many bistros hawking drinks.

Tyler's so attentive, making sure my drink's wrapped in an insulated cardboard holder, sweeping stray strands of hair from my face, even dabbing the side of the cup with a napkin so nothing drips on me.

I can't help but blush as I notice women darting glances our way, probably wondering why such a striking man is hooked up with me.

His entire focus is on me, as if I'm the only person in the universe. It feels so nice, so different from the way men treated me in the past. Hurried, rushed, one eye on their phone, like every minute was on the meter. But then again, I was that way too. Never one to take time out to smell the roses, walk in the rain with nothing to do but breathe.

"I enjoyed the afternoon and the treats." My voice comes out too whispery.

"Same here." He sweeps my hair aside, and right in the middle of the crowded shop, he zeroes in on my lips and kisses me.

Holy moly! His lips and mouth feel too good. I've never been ambushed by a man before. Never so unsuspecting and oblivious to his intention. Sure, I've only been staring at those lips while sampling the food, and yes, I'm partially melted by his invigorating, strong presence and the heat in his eyes, and the vision of us as a couple, strolling off into the sunset, or sailing on a yacht on warm, balmy seas.

But pounced on and kissed? This doesn't happen to Kelly Kennedy, the tough-nosed former investment banker, now, a scrappy, single mother who works two jobs.

He turns to deepen the kiss, and I gasp as he slides his tongue between my parted lips. He tastes sweet and fragrant, vanilla tea and almonds, but the scent of him is woodsy, strong, and stimulating, like leather, coffee, and musk.

My body reacts like a flash fire, and I'm hot, needy, and clingy, overwhelmed and engulfed by his spell.

Clap, clap, clap. Seems we have an audience, or maybe the other patrons want us to get a room.

Tyler doesn't jerk away from me like a guilty child caught with the cookies. He cups the side of my face and lingers, giving me one last soft peck.

"Lovely Kelly," he whispers. "Another time and another place."

Is that a promise or a hint of regret?

The sights and sounds of the busy bistro intrude as I back away. I can't help the feeling of awe of what just happened. No man, no where, has ever moved me, rearranged my heart and priorities and mind and goals in the space of a single kiss.

"What's wrong with the here and now?" I make an attempt at banter.

He leans in for another kiss and takes my hand. "Let's go somewhere and get Bree her present."

Chapter 9

~ Kelly ~

BREE IS OVER THE MOON excited when we return to my mom's apartment. She launches herself at Tyler through the doorway.

"Nana says you get us a big tree!"

My eyes dart to the corner near the fireplace. It's empty, although my mother's already pushed aside the winged chair and fake ficus tree to make room. She's probably talking about the old plastic tree she pulls out year after year. Some of the wires for the branches have been bent and unbent to the point of breaking.

Tyler allows Bree to hug his legs, but he doesn't pick her up. Good for him. He must know he needs permission from me before showing her affection.

I hoist Bree into my arms and tap her nose. "Why would Ty get you a tree? Nana already has one in the closet."

She crosses her little arms and juts her chin. "Nana says Father Chwistmas give big tree."

"Of course he does." I humor her and don't point out that Tyler is not Father Christmas, far from it.

Last year, before I was arrested and jailed, we had a Fraser fir tree and ornaments from Tiffany's in crystal and silver, trimmed with their signature robin's egg blue ribbons.

Mother waves a list in Tyler's face. "Jaden will drive all of us to the tree farm. While we're there, I have things for you to fix."

I know she's been wanting a son-in-law, but this is too much. Tyler is a virtual stranger.

"Wait, what's going on here?" I don't want to seem obvious, but if we're all going to the Christmas tree farm, Tyler will be alone in the apartment.

Mother blinks in a way that tells me she's up to something. "You're coming to the tree farm, aren't you? Bree wants a real tree, just like last year."

"That was in New York."

Bree squirms in my arms to be let down. "I want real tree. Nana pwo-mised."

"Sure, sweetie, wait here for a minute?" I need to speak to Mother in private, so I guide her toward the kitchen.

As soon as the door closes, I whisper, "Why's he fixing things in your apartment alone?"

"Someone has to stay behind with the roast in the oven." Mama crosses her arms and juts her chin the same way Bree did a few minutes earlier. "He agreed to help me out. It's a lot easier for a tall man to change light bulbs and smoke alarm batteries than for me or you to bring out the step ladder and struggle with it."

"Jaden can help." I refer to Ella's tall soccer goalkeeper boyfriend.

"Pfuh." Mama flaps her hand. "Jaden doesn't need the money. His parents own half of Silicon Valley."

"Oh, wait. Did you give him money already?"

"A small advance. I have lots I need worked on." Mother bobs her head. "Oh, I hear the door. That must be Jaden and Ella."

Of all the confounded interference. Steam practically hisses through my nostrils. I don't need her manipulation, as if it's not bad enough already with Bree fixated on Tyler.

I haven't even processed that kiss. What the heck was that about? After the Ferry building, Tyler and I walked along the Embarcadero and found a "Make Your Own Monster Puppet" kit for Bree. I also bought scented candles for Mother and a hairclip made with parrot plumage for Ella. Neither he, nor I, said half a word to each other on the way back, probably both lost in our thoughts. Talk about awkward.

Jaden pops into the kitchen with a stack of takeout containers. "You guys leaving now or will I have time to heat something up?"

"Go ahead. Bree needs to go potty and get her gear on." I follow Mother out of the kitchen.

"Mama, come on, come on." Bree bounces, tugging my hand.

Ella finishes snapping the buttons on Bree's jacket and pats her head. "You get to pick the tree. Ready?"

"Except she needs to potty." I can't believe I have to undo the jacket and rain pants, but my sister's not a mother so what does she know about getting a child ready for an outing?

I don't dare look at Tyler. He's staring at the family pictures in front of the fireplace. This is all too cozy, like he belongs here with us.

I walk Bree past him toward the bathroom. A loud popping and hissing sound comes from the kitchen.

"Get down." Tyler lunges at Bree, knocks her to the ground, and crouches behind the couch, his hands in position as if around a machine gun.

Bree's head thumps the floor, and she let's out a yelp.

My baby! I rush to pick her up and check her head.

"Owie, owie," she says, but I can tell she's not hurt as much as startled. "I have a big bump like in the cartoons."

I peek at Tyler. He stands frozen behind the couch, his fists clenched and his posture slumped. He has to go past all of us to get to the front door, and I bet he's hoping we don't notice him as he slinks out.

"What happened?" Mother opens the kitchen door. "Did something blow up?"

Jaden steps out with a plate of sausage and rice. "That was the microwave."

"I saw everything," Ella says. "Tyler freaked out when the sausage popped. He was protecting Bree."

Refraining from a snide remark, I rub Bree's head to see if she's hurt. Tyler must be mortified. How horrible it is for him to not be in complete control of his actions. But however bad I feel for him, I can't risk my daughter's safety. What if he went into a full blown panic attack and thought she was the enemy?

He moves past me and Bree, his face still downcast. "I'm sorry. I have to go now."

"Oh no, you don't." Mother corrals him near the door. "It's quite all right. Everyone's fine. Besides, I paid you already for the handyman stuff. So you still have your list to do."

"You sure?" Tyler rubs the back of his neck. His eyes light up, as if hoping against hope that everyone would think he's normal.

"Of course. I'll also need you to pull the candlesticks out from the storage unit downstairs and polish them." Mother smiles and pats his arm. "After you're done with that, we should be back with the tree, and you can help us with the lights and ornaments."

Ugh. I don't get Mother. Is she so kind hearted she wants him to feel useful, or is she still trying to play Cupid? And seriously, I don't see how she can leave him alone in her apartment. If a popping microwave can freak him out, what's to say we don't come back and find him setting fire to the place because he saw enemy combatants?

That does it. If Tyler's staying, I'll have to stick around to make sure he's safe.

"Bree?" I kiss her and smooth her hair. "Mama's going to stay here and help Ty clean Nana's place. You stay with Auntie Ella, okay? No running off."

"No running off. I pwo-mise. Santa says if I good girl, I get a papa for Chwistmas."

Chapter 10

~ Tyler ~

TYLER GRITTED HIS TEETH AND straightened his spine as he watched Kelly kiss Bree and wave goodbye to her family. Peggy flashed him an A-OK hand sign, and he had no choice but to stick around and finish the job.

Not that he'd ever run from his problems. Nope. A real man faced everything square on, and he'd screwed up. Even though he'd taken his medicine, he'd allowed himself to get excited and carried away with Kelly and the kiss. There was no excuse.

Tyler moved away from the door and unhooked the keys to the storage locker. "I'm going to fetch your mother's candlesticks. Anything you need out there?"

Kelly glared at him, as if finally noticing the white elephant in the room. "I don't know what you and my mother agreed to. Sounds like she has you doing jobs for her on a regular basis?"

"Pretty much. I mean, she's already paid me. I can give it back. I don't mean to scam off your mom." He fished a wad of bills from his pocket. "I spent some of it, but I'll pay her back every penny."

"Don't." Kelly backed away from him. "I'm serious. Take the money and let's go through her list before they return. I know my mother, and she has to have everything arranged exactly the way she wants."

"Sure, okay, let's get to it." Tyler left the money on the counter behind the mail and followed Kelly to the storage locker.

For the next hour or so, they polished the candlesticks, pulled out boxes of ornaments, and set them on the coffee table for the tree trimming. Kelly popped popcorn, infusing the kitchen with a fresh scent, while Tyler changed the alarm batteries and made sure every light bulb was functioning.

The sound of the popcorn popping didn't disturb him because he expected it, knew it was happening. It was the surprises that short circuited his conscious mind, bringing back the sights, sounds, and odors of the war zone: falling mortar, cracked windows, and mangled bodies.

Kelly handed him a needle and string and placed a bowl of raw cranberries between them. "Did you guys do this when you were little?"

"We had popcorn, but no cranberries."

"No cranberries?" Kelly popped one in her mouth and made a sour face. "How boring."

"My mother buttered and salted the popcorn too, so we ate more than we strung."

"Oh, I'll bet. Did your father take you tree shopping or did you guys cut one down from whatever farm you grew up in?"

He poked through a fat cranberry, squirting some of the juice over his fingers and tied a knot. "My father took me out with a saw whenever he was home. My uncle had a tree farm, and he'd let me pick a tree. Only catch, I had to saw it down, and that's hard work."

"That's where you got all the muscles." Kelly laughed as she wrapped a half-strung garland around his bicep. Her perfume and the closeness of her body heat knocked Tyler's heartbeat up a notch.

He cleared his throat. "I wonder what's taking them so long."

Kelly dropped the garland on the kitchen table and ran her hand up his forearm along the tail of his tattoo. "I bet Bree can't make up her mind. Last year, I had Tiffany's deliver a tree completely trimmed and decorated, and she was upset because she wanted to do it herself."

"Tiffany's? Like in New York?" Tyler struggled to keep his voice steady. If she kept trailing her fingers like that, he'd be justified in bending her over for a long, slow kiss.

As if aware of his thoughts, Kelly flushed and fanned herself. "Anyway, that was last year and this is this year. She wasn't old enough to string popcorn and stuff."

Strange. All Tyler knew about Tiffany's was the movie *Breakfast at Tiffany's* and that it was an expensive jewelry store. Maybe Kelly referred to a friend of hers who prepared Christmas trees.

"Where did you grow up?" he asked, keeping his tone casual since Kelly didn't seem forthcoming about her background.

"Massachusetts."

"You related to the famous Kennedys?" He'd seen her mother's name on the envelopes she left lying around.

"Not a chance." Kelly plucked a handful of popcorn and laid them in a row.

"So, what made you move to California?" His garland was longer than hers and more colorful, since he alternated cranberries and popcorn.

"Mom's out here. I want to be close to family."

Made sense, except her eyes dodged his, and her shoulders slumped in a closed position.

She definitely had something to hide.

~ Kelly ~

What's with the twenty questions? I check the clock, wondering why my family's not back. It's been two hours already. Knowing Mom, she's purposely leaving me and Tyler alone. Although after that kiss earlier, I'm salivating every time he comes closer. The episode with Bree seems to have sobered him up, and he's being ultra careful to be a gentleman. He hadn't even responded when I admired his ink and muscles.

My head's in a fog, and I need coffee. Tyler's being friendly, trying to keep things light. He's homeless so he probably doesn't have internet, and he won't find out about my arrest and conviction, not unless someone tells him. But he's a trained warrior, and my being spooked has him suspicious.

I plaster a wide smile and stretch with my hands above my head. "I need a cup of coffee. How about you?"

"Sure we can take a break? I still have to detangle the lights."

"You work too hard." I punch his shoulder lightly and scoot around him to the coffeemaker. He turns and I end up brushing against him as I round the corner of the kitchen table.

I gasp at the spark of electricity arcing between us. He must have felt it too, because his blue eyes darken from Tiffany shade to a deep navy. The garland he's working on drops, sliding to the table, and he feathers the backs of his fingers over my cheek.

All I can think about is his hard, muscular body, and the way his lips burned through mine, as if he'd hungered for a million years, yet holding back and taking his sweet time. I lean into his touch and rest my hands on his waist, feeling him tense.

"What's going on here?" Tyler's voice is tight, barely rasping. "I shouldn't ... This is wrong."

I swallow the drool collecting under my tongue. Does he not feel it? Is he not affected by me?

"Why?" My hands slide up his sides and he shudders, sucking in his breath. I honestly can't remember the last time a man had me so mesmerized. His scent is sexy and woodsy, sending heat spiraling through me and making it hard to think.

His gaze lowers to my lips. “I can’t help but want to kiss you, but you’re suspicious.”

The hairs on the back of my scalp bristle. He’s right. I *am* suspicious, but not of his motives. He can’t help the situation he’s in, and he doesn’t want anyone’s pity.

God help me, he’s hot, here, and wants to kiss me.

I pull my arms around him and press myself against him. “I can’t help it either. Kiss me.”

This time, I step up on tippy toes and inhale his hot breath before tapping his lips with mine. He responds immediately, his fingers streaking through my hair as he slants his head and covers my mouth with his.

I open up to him, stroking his tongue, drinking him in. Desire stokes in my lower abdomen and tingly flutters wrap around my shoulders.

A moan escapes me when Tyler deepens the kiss, his hands weaving possessively through my hair. The sheer power of his strength and the fierceness of his hunger sets me on fire.

What am I doing? I can’t fight this. Don’t want to. Don’t let this end.

Bang. Voices intrude. They’re back. Crap. I stiffen to ease myself out of the kiss, but Tyler doesn’t let go.

His lips and tongue continue to work their magic, melting me with liquid pleasure. One more touch, another caress. I suck on his lower lip and squeeze the cords of his shoulders.

“Kelly. We got mistletoe.” Mother’s voice rings through the kitchen door.

I push away from Tyler in the nick of time.

“Mama!” Bree exclaims as she careens into the kitchen. “We got a big tree, and Nana bought a big gold star. I get to put it on, please, please.”

She shoves a gilded star, still in its package at me. “I want Santa to see the star and give me a real papa.”

She's not looking at Tyler. This is progress. As long as she thinks it's not Tyler, I have a chance for a little fun, maybe more.

Chapter 11

~ Tyler ~

THE RESINY FRAGRANCE OF THE Christmas tree filled the room, and a fire crackled in the fireplace. Christmas carols played on the stereo. The Kennedy family frolicked around the tree admiring the ornaments which brought back fond memories.

Tyler took a sip of spiced apple cider and closed his eyes, remembering his favorite ornaments, his Baby's First Christmas star, the teddy bear caboose, and his set of Army men. He wasn't even sure his mother had kept anything after his father died. They'd lost the farm and moved to a dingy apartment, too small for trees, parties, and fun.

"Who wants to put up the star?" Peggy held up the golden star ornament. "I can't reach it."

"Me, me, me!" Bree jumped and clapped, grasping for it.

"But you can't reach it either." Peggy jiggled Bree's cheek. "You picked a big old tree."

Kelly leaned over the back of the sofa and squeezed his shoulders. "Penny for your thoughts? You seem to be far away."

He set the mug of cider on the coffee table and whispered, "Do you mind if I help Bree put up the star?"

"Go ahead, and thanks for asking."

His consideration earned him a smile, one which seemed to wrap him in a warm blanket. He wanted Kelly, wished things could be different. Emotions flooded him along with images of them in a mountain cabin huddled in a thick down comforter.

Bree tapped his knees, breaking his train of thought. "Ty, pick me up. I wanna put the star."

"Okay, missy." Tyler lifted her and stood at the same time, placing her onto his shoulders.

"Whee! That's fun. Do it again." Bree grabbed his hair with one hand and bounced on the back of his neck.

"The star first."

"Wait, wait." Peggy waved for Ella and Jaden to gather around. "Who wants to do the reading?"

"I will." Kelly reached for the Bible. "Or Tyler, do you want to?"

"Sure." Tyler maneuvered himself to Kelly's side while she held the Bible and pointed to the passages. "When they had heard the king, they departed; and, lo, the star, which they saw in the east, went before them, till it came and stood over where the young child was. When they saw the star, they rejoiced with exceeding great joy. And when they were come into the house, they saw the young child with Mary his mother, and fell down, and worshipped him: and when they had opened their treasures, they presented unto him gifts; gold, and frankincense and myrrh."

"Bree, what does the star stand for?" Peggy shook Bree's chubby little foot.

"Jesus!" she squealed. "It's his birthday."

"Right. We should be like that star and lead people to Christ."

"Yay." Bree bounced and squirmed. "I get to put the star up."

Tyler's heart warmed as he lifted Bree up high and held her. She was so trusting, and when she was finished, he turned her in his arms and hugged her.

"You'll never get rid of her now," Ella said as she shut off the video camera.

"What do you mean?"

"I want Ty to throw me up and catch me," Bree said.

"Hope you like the workout." Kelly pinched his waist. "What? No love handles? We're going to have to fix that, won't we? Ready to eat?"

~ Kelly ~

"So, what's going on between you and Tyler?" Ella and I are elbows deep in dishwater. Mother's annual tree-trimming dinner was a rousing success, and Tyler must have eaten enough for an entire team of football players. After dessert, Tyler and Jaden took Mother and Bree out for a stroll to work off the calories.

"Nothing yet." I hand her a plate. "He's attractive."

"Understatement of the year. He's a frickin hunk, and the thing is, he doesn't think he's hot."

"He has his issues." I'm pretty sure Mother's updated Ella on everything, filling in the gaps with speculation and embellishments. "I'm not sure why Mom insists on including him. I mean, Bree might get the wrong idea."

"Which is?" Ella stacks the dried dish onto a pile.

"I'm sure you heard about her obsession for finding her father."

"Oh, yes. Over and over from both Bree and Mom. But honestly, I think you should be thinking about yourself instead of what Mom and Bree want."

I juggle a glass, almost dropping it. "I'm not interested in dating. I have my daughter. I'm going to get my career back. I don't need distractions. Especially a guy who has fits. You saw what he did with Bree?"

"Yeah, but he didn't really hurt her. He just has quick reflexes."

"He has post traumatic stress disorder. He takes psych meds, goes to therapy." *And his kisses are out of this world. And he's kind and protective and honorable. Argh.*

"Everyone has problems." Ella slaps me with a dishtowel. "Does he know you've been in jail?"

"Shhh ..." I look over my shoulder. Thankfully they're not back. "I'm ashamed of what I did. Anyway, he doesn't need to know. It's not like we're in a relationship or anything."

"Keep saying that." Ella quirks her eyebrow. "All I see are sparks flying between you two. It's like the air is charged with lightning, and you can't keep your hands or eyes off each other. You looked so guilty when we got back from Christmas tree shopping."

My face heats from her teasing tone. "We weren't done with the garlands. You know how Mom is."

Ella giggles. "Of course you weren't done, because you were otherwise occupied. I bet he's an awesome kisser."

"Who's an awesome kisser?" Jaden's voice sneaks up behind us.

"How'd you get back without us hearing?" Ella jumps to her tippy toes and kisses him.

Their smacks and smooches are loud and exaggerated. I turn the water to full blast and scrub the roasting pan.

Tyler's a homeless vet. Tyler has PTSD. Tyler's unemployed. Tyler's a free spirit. If Tyler gets back on his feet, he'll have a million women after him. Tyler's not for me, and I don't need him. But I can't help wanting him. What's wrong with me?

"Whee!" Bree squeals. "Throw me again."

And he's so good with Bree. What's not to like?

"One more time. Ty needs a rest." Even the star athlete sounds out of breath. Well, Bree can do that, for sure.

I glance at the clock. It's way past Bree's bedtime. Time to be the bad guy. Wiping my hands on my apron, I cross to the living room.

"That was fun, wasn't it?" I hold out my hands for Bree.

A relieved looking Tyler hands her over and wipes the hair off his forehead. "She's a ball of energy."

I make a show of sniffing her. "You need a bath, missy."

"No, I don't. I smell like Ty."

Uh, well, there's his cologne on her, mixed with dirt, peppermint candy, and fruit snacks.

"Say bye bye to Ty. It's bath time." I remove her boots and hang up her jacket.

Bree hugs onto Tyler's knees. "Want Ty to give me bath."

"Sorry, Ty has to leave." I take her hand, but she slaps herself on the ground.

"No, leave. No. No. No." Her face scrunches beet red, and she lets out a howl. "I want Ty to be my papa."

"We already went over this." I drag her off the floor. "Ty's not your father. You don't have a father. You don't need a father."

Bree wails louder. "I want Ty to be papa. Give me a bath and read me stories."

"No, you don't." Pressure explodes over my temples, and my head throbs. "Mama will give you a bath and Nana reads you stories or Auntie Ella."

"No. No. No." She's beyond reasoning. "I want Papa tuck me in. I pwayed real hard and Santa pwo-mised."

"Nana has a surprise for you," Mother says, squeezing a rubber duckie. "It's in the bathroom."

"Want papa." Bree kicks and struggles toward Tyler's direction. Tears bathe her face, and she's crying as if her heart is breaking.

I yank her into the bathroom. She's in full meltdown mode, and it takes all my strength to pull off her clothes and put her into the bathtub.

Thankfully her exhaustion overcomes her will, and after splashing and pouting and kicking, she eventually gives up. After I pull her out of the tub and dress her, I carry her to the bed she uses when visiting my mother.

"I want my papa," she lisps before tucking her thumb in her mouth. A tiny tear trails down the side of her chubby cheek, and her lips quiver.

"I'm sorry, babe. I'm so sorry." I kiss her. Maybe I was wrong to conceive her through artificial means. Maybe I was selfish and foolish, to think she wouldn't care.

I wipe a tear from my eye and kneel at the side of her bed to pray.

Chapter 12

~ Tyler ~

TYLER FOUND SAWYER AT THE Embarcadero station in his usual spot. "How's business this morning?"

"Cranking. It's the week before Christmas." He strummed a few bars of a bluesy version of "Rocking Around the Christmas Tree." "You get lucky?"

Tyler handed him the Performance Necklace. "If lucky means a family dinner, trimming the tree, and bouncing a four-year-old through Golden Gate Park, then yes, I did."

"Yeah, yeah. What about the girl?"

"Cute. Like I said, she's a ball of energy. Wore me out." He rubbed his sore shoulders and twisted his arms over his head to stretch.

"Woot, woot. Magic Necklace." Sawyer reattached it around his neck. "I'm ready to get some action tonight."

Tyler felt his face heat. "I wasn't talking about Kelly. She was nice, but I kinda get the feeling she's holding back. I don't blame her. I don't have a job or anything. I'm just a bum her mother picked up to do some work."

"It doesn't have to be this way," Sawyer said, setting his guitar aside. "You can gig with me. I know a few bar owners. They let me play weeknights. With your star power, we'd be packing them in."

Tyler's chest constricted. It wasn't the singing in public as much as the boisterous crowds, the flashing lights, and the unexpected fights breaking out.

"I'd rather sing in church, but they don't pay."

"And even if they did, you'd give it all to Warspring." Sawyer opened his guitar case. "I picked up your mail. They sent you a calendar and an invitation to their annual Donor's Christmas party."

"Gee, thanks," Tyler said. "I gotta get going and pick up some tips."

When Tyler was out of sight of Sawyer, he opened the invitation. Smiling children dressed in their native garb greeted him. He smiled, his heart warming.

Warspring was a classy organization with aid groups in all the global hotspots. They kept expenses to a minimum in order to funnel most of the money to the children, but every Christmas they held a donor appreciation bash. He'd never attended before since he'd been overseas, and he couldn't see himself rubbing shoulders with the snooty self-satisfied millionaires who frequented such events. But still, they'd given him Gold level for his contributions, and it entitled him to bring a guest and meet the founder's family.

He stepped out of the BART station and walked toward the Ferry Building. Now that the rain had stopped, groomers were resurfacing the outdoor ice rink while lines of children and their parents waited. He scanned the crowd briefly, wondering if Kelly would bring Bree.

He hadn't had a chance to say goodbye to her last night since she was busy with an overtired but cranky toddler. Even though her family had urged him to stop by again, and her mother had thought of more work for him to do, Tyler wondered if he'd overstayed his welcome. Bree was getting too attached to him, and he was sure Kelly wasn't pleased. She'd barely looked at him while corralling her daughter, and her words made it clear what she thought about the prospect.

Ty's not your father. You don't have a father. You don't need a father.

She got part of it right. No one needed a father without a job, one who could take off as the whim struck. The only reason he was in San Francisco was because Warspring International had offices there and he had a proposal for them.

He wandered up and down the street, walking past the lobby of an old multi-tenanted office building. Would anyone be in on a Sunday? Was his plan foolish? How many weeks had he hung around this neighborhood thinking and rethinking? It could work, should work.

He glanced up. The curtains were open on the fifth floor where Warspring had their offices. Even if no one was in, he could at least case the joint. Wiping his sweaty palms down the sides of his jeans, he checked his shirt in the reflection of the mirrored door and stepped into the lobby. *Remember, walk tall, act as if you belong. You're a donor. Look like you own the place.*

He took the elevator to the Warspring suite. The door wasn't locked, so he entered the lobby. The walls were plastered with panels of photographs. Tyler shuddered at the haunted eyes and listless faces. He was drawn to the rows of Afghan children, their faces smeared with dirt and cuts, their gray-green eyes dull and old, etched with experiences no child should have to endure.

"May I help you?" a young Asian woman emerged from one of the offices. "Our receptionist is on vacation."

"Sure, thanks." He shook her offered hand firmly. "I'd like to talk to the program director."

The woman wrinkled her forehead. "Do you have an appointment?"

"No, ma'am. I was in the neighborhood and thought I'd take a chance."

She tapped the desk, scrutinizing him. "You look familiar. Where have I seen you before?"

Maybe she'd passed him in the subway or spied him hanging out with Sawyer. She'd know he was a homeless vet and throw him out.

Tyler braced himself, but forced a grin. "I do have that kind of ordinary face you see a lot around here."

"You're kidding, right?" She waved him to the office. "I'm Carina Chen, the director of finance and fundraising."

"Tyler Manning. I should have introduced myself earlier."

She snapped her fingers. "Of course. Mr. Manning, one of our faithful donors. You've been in the news lately. Have a seat. Want anything to drink? Juice, tea?"

"I'm good, well, actually if you have juice, I'll take it." After all, he hadn't had breakfast. Despite the large dinner he had the night before, he was hungry.

"I'll be right back." She hustled from her office, leaving Tyler to stare at the electronic photo frame on her desk. It cycled through the various trips she'd taken and the aid agencies she'd visited.

She returned bearing a tray of bagels and jams. Setting the juice in front of him, she said, "Our program director's not here. Maybe you can tell me what you want and I'll pass it on to him."

"Sure." He cleared his throat. "I'm a veteran back from Afghanistan, and I'm especially interested in the orphans left behind. I know there's a crying need for the girls to be housed and educated, but I feel the boys need attention too."

She folded her arms across the desk. "We fund orphanages that take in both boys and girls. Why would you think they'd be neglected?"

"I didn't mean it that way. I guess I should have written a proposal or something, but hear me out." Tyler sat straighter and leaned forward. "Their physical needs are taken care of, but they don't have father figures. As soon as they're old enough to leave, they're left to their own and end up in one of the militias or gangs."

"True, but I don't see how we can change that." Carina rubbed her chin. "We try to give them an education, but as you know, life's difficult in the refugee camps, and the orphanages are overcrowded. It's hard to shield them from the allures of fighting."

"I was thinking sports programs. Soccer, basketball, volleyball, team sports that build sportsmanship and give them healthy competition. If we can get them while they're young, and show them how to cooperate as well as compete, give them healthy outlets ..."

"We're already stretched thin," Carina said. "You have a good point, but I'm afraid people will think sports is a luxury. You know, given the choice between feeding an additional thousand mouths versus providing them with sports facilities, not to mention coaches."

"The costs won't be too high. Just a ball, a net or field." Sweat dampened Tyler's brow. "It'll give them an outlet to channel their energy in a healthy way."

Carina woke the laptop sitting on her table. "It's a great idea if we had additional funds."

"I can help. Maybe I can go door to door and solicit donations?"

She tilted the laptop screen. "See this? Here are the budget shortfalls we have on our existing programs. I've been looking to cut costs. I even wanted to do away with the annual Donor's Ball, but Dylan, the director, said no way. I mean, you could go door to door, but we'll need a solicitor's permit. Frankly, I'm not sure you alone could raise the kind of cash needed to fund a new program. The pitch to give more money to boys falls on deaf ears. People are more interested in the plight of girls and women."

"Girls can play sports too."

She chuckled. "In America, yes. But not in Afghanistan. You know they seclude girls from a certain age upward? We have to run a network of home schools with female teachers to meet with them. There's not going to be a women's basketball team in Afghanistan anytime soon."

"What's this about a women's basketball team?" A jolly voice sounded from the lobby.

Carina blushed and her eyelashes fluttered when she looked up. Tyler recognized Dylan Jewell, the director and son of the founder, from the picture in the glossy invitation. Without acknowledging Tyler, Dylan bent over the desk and kissed Carina on the lips.

Tyler swallowed and pushed his chair back. They'd dismissed him. The idea was harebrained. Even Sawyer thought so. Help boys in Afghanistan so they could grow up and fight. Hadn't it been a boy strapped with IEDs who'd blown up his buddies?

It took a moment for Tyler to realize Dylan was speaking to him.

"I hear you're proposing sports programs for Afghan youths at the camps and orphanages." Dylan sat on the corner of Carina's desk.

"Yes, low cost sports. Basketball, soccer, volleyball. It'll improve the mental outlook for the kids. Some of them could graduate to becoming coaches or managers for the teams."

"Not a bad idea at all." Dylan stroked his jaw. It looked like he was growing a beard. "Carina's always worried about cash flow, but she says you're willing to put yourself out there to raise funds."

"I would definitely increase my contribution if I could, knowing it'll go to this program. I've been there and have seen the faces of the youth. They're tired of war and need something to look forward to." Heck, he'd get a job if it would mean more money for his program.

Dylan offered his hand. "Let's shake on it. You up your contribution, and I'll have Carina run the numbers and contact the orphanages and refugee camps."

Behind him, Carina made a funny face. "Starting a new program isn't that simple. We'll need ongoing commitments and a plan for the increased expenditures, not to mention the approval of the board. I'm not sure we can meet the new obligation."

"Not if we bring Mr. Manning on as spokesman." Dylan smirked as if the brilliant idea were his. "Ex-Stanford quarterback, Raiders pro-pick, decorated veteran. Think of the story. He's been there, fought them, and cares for the children of his enemies."

"Yeah, but how much can he raise going door to door?" Carina scowled, her pretty little eyebrows narrowing.

"No one said anything about door to door." Dylan chuckled. "We're talking media appearances, ads, and speaking engagements, appearing at my concerts."

"Whoa, wait." Tyler's gaze bounced between Dylan and Carina. He hadn't meant for this to get out of hand. All of this sounded like crowds, loud noises, screaming, shouting, and melees.

"That's right." Carina slapped the desk. "I'm already overworked. You have me managing your band, coordinating the fundraising, and doing the books. That's three jobs, and now you're asking me to put together a new program structure?"

"Hire someone for whatever's your least favorite job." Dylan snagged her around the shoulders and rubbed her back.

"But we can't afford—"

He cut her off with another wet, slurpy kiss. Hadn't these two heard of private displays of affection?

"It's the end of the year," Dylan said after they emerged for air. "Let's make a big push for donations. Two priorities. I want a new program that makes Warspring stand out from all the aid organizations, and I want you to hire an assistant. Lay off the receptionist if you have to. She's never around."

"But she's your sister's friend."

"Yeah, and she acts like it too." Dylan tweaked Carina's nose. "I think she's spying on us for my father."

Tyler shifted in his seat. He didn't need to hear any of this. Had they forgotten his presence? Should he slide out of his chair and make a discreet exit?

A firm hand clamped on his shoulder.

"Leaving so soon?" Dylan Jewell wasn't a man who expected to be ignored. "Let's start over with the introductions. I'm Dylan Jewell, program director of

Warspring International, and this is Carina Chen, my sidekick."

That comment earned him a puckered face and a punch.

Tyler shook Dylan's hand. "Tyler Manning."

"Great. What do you think about being our spokesman? You've been in the news lately and frankly, you have a great story behind it all."

"Assuming he'll do motivational speaking ..." Carina fiddled with a spreadsheet. "This could work. How much per plate can we charge with Tyler on the agenda?"

"Depends on the story and the pitch," Dylan said. "So, Tyler, what do you say?"

"Uh, well ..." What excuse could he give? That he was afraid of crowds and loud noises? Kelly wouldn't respect him if he allowed his fears to rule him.

Feeling as if he'd stepped off the edge of a cliff, he replied. "When do I start?"

Slap. Dylan's hand landed on his back, followed by a bear hug. "Tonight. I'm doing a presentation at a business leaders' dinner. You can say a few words."

"Anything in particular?"

"Whatever you want. I'm sure you have many stories about your time in Afghanistan, or what motivated you to go from football to the Army, or even better, your vision for the sports program for Afghan orphans."

Carina moved to the other side of Tyler, hemming him in. "I'll have the contracts drawn up. How about we go to lunch and discuss terms?"

Vinnie and Babycakes with brass knuckles couldn't have done a better job.

"Great, I'm your man."

Chapter 13

~ Kelly ~

"YOU HAVE TO GIVE HIS money back," Mother says, shoving the wad of bills Tyler left into my purse.

"Why me? You're the one who hired him." I'm running late already. "Thanks for watching Bree, but if I don't get to my shift, I won't make it to evening service."

"You're singing the special. Be early."

"Exactly, which is why I don't have time to hunt Tyler down."

"Come on, we both know this is the best excuse for talking to him again. He was sorry about Bree's tantrum, and I get the feeling he won't be coming back. I tried to offer him another job—"

"Mom, really, it might be better if he doesn't see Bree again."

"I agree," Mother says, surprising me. "But that doesn't mean you can't go out with him without Bree around. I can watch her anytime, you know."

"Well, maybe. I really have to go." I kiss her. "When Bree wakes up, don't forget to brush her teeth. We skipped last night. Bye!"

Try as I might, I can't get Tyler out of my mind. It's not his fault Bree has such an obsession about him. He's easy going, fun, with big, strong shoulders. And he needs the money. But where in this crowded city will I find him? It's not like I can hang around at the shopping center hoping he'll wander by.

I take the BART to the Embarcadero station, the place Tyler had his PTSD episode. Traffic's light on Sunday.

Powerwalking past several panhandlers, I emerge from the platform and look around. A man with a guitar sits on a crate in front of an open guitar case.

"Lady, sing you a carol? How about 'Jingle Bell Rock?'"

I barely glance at the big black man, except he's wearing a beaded necklace with a Chinese coin, just like the one Tyler had on last night. He looks vaguely familiar.

That's it. He's the guy who was interviewed after he stun gunned Tyler.

Walking back, I ask, "Sir, would you happen to know Tyler Manning?"

The man's mouth breaks into a large smile as his eyes rove over me. Not that there's much to see. I'm wearing jeans and an old sweatshirt, my cleaning job attire.

"Women ask me that all the time," the man replies. He holds out his hand. "Sawyer McGee."

I take his hand and give him a hefty shake. "Do you know Tyler or not?"

"Now, now, now." Sawyer grins and wags a finger. "I can't be giving out information without knowing who you are, what your place of business is, and three references, preferably from little old ladies you help cross the street or retired clergymen."

"I don't have time for this." I'm pretty sure he's a friend of Tyler's, but if he's going to ask me a hundred questions and butt his nose into my business, I'm out of here.

"Tyler never mentioned you were so rude." The man's melodious voice drifts behind me.

"Excuse me?" I snap my head around and head back his direction. "I asked you a simple question and you want to drag this into a social interaction. I'm going to be late for work as it is."

He quirks his eyebrows as if trying to figure me out. "You're Bree's mom, aren't you? The one who wore him out."

"Yes, I am. And since you do know Tyler, kindly let him know I have his money."

"Money, as in moolah?" Sawyer's mouth widens and his eyes light. "I can give it to him."

"No, can do. I have to work right now, but tell Tyler I'll be outside of the Mogul Bank building at five when my shift ends."

"You know, lady, I don't have to tell him anything." Sawyer strums a jangled chord. "You're wasting my time. I've got songs to sing and bills to pay."

Yeah, right. He wants a tip. I extract a five and drop it in his case. "You can sing 'Santa I've Been Naughty' for me. And Sawyer, I'm sorry for being rude. Please let Tyler know I'm looking for him."

"Sure thing. Name?"

"Kelly."

"Number?" He unlocks his cell phone. "I'll text you when I give him the message. You can call me anytime, you know. You want Tyler, I'm your man."

I don't know what his game is, but he's my only link to Tyler right now, and I'm not ready to give him up. Will I ever?

I type my number into Sawyer's phone. "Call me when Tyler gets the message. I don't want to wait around forever since it gets dark early this time of year."

~ Tyler ~

Tyler said goodbye to Dylan and Carina and headed for the BART station.

He had a job and a purpose. He'd get a salary to oversee the fundraising venues and line up speakers and events. In addition, Warspring would pay him a thousand dollars per speaking engagement and include traveling and lodging expenses. He'd even convinced Dylan that rock concerts were not conducive to gathering donations and suggested speaking to sports teams and business executives instead.

Sawyer was at his post, sipping a soda. "Hey, my man. Get big tips today?"

"Even better." Tyler fist bumped him. "You're looking at the new speaker for Warspring International. I'm going to be raising funds at charity banquets and special events."

"Woohoo! That's awesome. How much are they paying?"

"Enough for me to triple my contributions and get my own program going. Remember we talked about sports for Afghan teens?"

"Uh, yeah. They bought it? I thought blankets and food were more important."

"That only feeds the body, not the soul. We need to give the youth healthy outlooks to life, optimism, and hope for the future. Sports is the answer."

Sawyer clapped a hand on his shoulder. "I can't believe I'm hearing you say that. Man, this is awesome."

"Even better, I get extra tickets to the Donor's Ball, and you're coming. Maybe you can audition for the band or find a job. They're also looking for an assistant for their finance director."

Actually, Kelly could use the job, but he should offer Sawyer a first shot.

"Guitar I can play, but no spreadsheets for me." Sawyer scratched his head. "But hey, that lady friend of yours was looking for you."

"Kelly? She was here?" The day kept getting better and better.

"In the flesh. Looking hot and bothered. Kind of rude at first, all business. She wants you to meet her outside of the Mogul Bank building where she works. You know where it is?"

"Near Mission Street Plaza in the Financial District. What time did she say she got off from work?"

"Five. I told her you were desperate to see her, worshipping the ground she walked on, mooning over her and unable to sleep."

"Shut it." Tyler shoved his friend lightly to conceal the happiness bubbling inside of him. "How about you put your guitar away and have a drink on me? I got a sign-on bonus, and we still have a couple hours to kill."

"Forget the drinks. Let's go shopping. You got to look the part of Mr. Executive Speaker."

Chapter 14

~ Kelly ~

I EMPTY MY GARBAGE CAN into the trash compactor and throw my rags into the washer. I'm grimy from cleaning out the refrigerator and emptying bottles of urine from the intern bullpen. I don't know what's with these bankers pissing in bottles instead of going to the bathroom. Maybe they didn't want to miss a single trade. But seriously, these days they have smartphones.

Back in my time, there was a girl who ended up with an intestinal disorder because she never went to the bathroom. She ended up lying on the floor in her office with her laptop because she was in such pain. But it was worth it. She got the return offer and is now a director.

I tidy up my cleaning supplies and lock the janitor's closet. Sawyer hasn't texted me so it's unlikely I'll see Tyler. Which is for the better since I'm sweaty and need a nice, long shower. I tie a bandana around my hair and pull on my winter jacket.

A cold breeze whips when I step out of the Mogul Bank building. Keeping my head down, I slide past a group of young bankers with their model playmates.

"Kelly?" A woman's voice calls from behind me. "I can't believe it's you."

It's Rebecca, my college roommate. Her heels clip clop on the sidewalk at a fast pace. She's wearing her signature Armani suit and Christian Louboutin pumps with the shiny red soles. Her blood-colored Hermès purse is easily worth fifty thousand, and her ears drip with Tiffany diamonds. She opens her arms as if to hug me.

"So nice to see you," she squeals. "I can't believe you're in San Francisco. When did they let you out of prison? It must have been horrible."

"Wasn't a tea party, but it was only a few months. Judge felt sorry for me for losing all my money." My eyes dart around, but the male interns don't seem to notice us. They're passing a bottle around and getting into a limo.

"They set you up," Rebecca said. "Whoever gave you the tip set you up and executed the opposite trade. Why didn't you check with me? I could have told you."

"It's old news now. So how've you been? I hear you're doing well."

She smooths her multicolored auburn-red hair. "Couldn't be better. We should have a drink sometime. How's your little girl?"

"She's a gem. The only thing important in my life."

Rebecca flings a smile my direction, except her gaze travels over my shoulder. That come hither look can't be for me.

"Well, hello-o there," she says to someone behind me.

Tyler walks over, his hands in his pockets. He's wearing a black leather jacket over a white dress shirt and pleated black dress pants. My breath catches in my throat. If I didn't know better, I'd think he was one of the bankers strolling toward the building.

Tyler nods to greet Rebecca, but his eyes are on me. "Kelly, are you done with work?"

"Uh, yes," I mumble, wishing I could disappear along with my bandana, holey jeans, and rain jacket. "I ran into a friend. Rebecca, this is Tyler. Tyler, Rebecca."

Rebecca holds her hand limp wristed to shake, or more likely offering it to Tyler to kiss.

He shakes it instead. "Nice to meet you. I hope I'm not interrupting anything."

"Oh, not at all," Rebecca says. "I was just asking Kelly about her darling Bree. Kelly, I'm glad to see you're back on your feet. If you ever need anything, a reference or a lead, call me. Let's do lunch sometime."

"Sure, anytime you're free." I stare at the sidewalk as Rebecca departs.

"Sawyer says you wanted to meet me here." Tyler takes my hand. "Shall we have dinner?"

"No. I mean, I'm not dressed, and I have to pick up Bree and go home. I only wanted to give you the money you left at my mom's place. Then I have church." I'm so jittery, my words come out in a flurry.

He takes my other hand and stares me square in the face. "I don't need the money."

"But you earned it."

"It's okay. I've got great news." His grin beams over his face, crinkling his eyes. "I got a job."

"Wow! That's wonderful." I throw my arms around him and bounce up and down. "What will you be doing?"

"Charity work, motivational speaking, and fundraising."

"I'm so happy for you. Does that mean you'll get off the streets?"

"Uh, no. I don't need a place to live, but when I travel, they'll include hotels and travel expenses." His mood seems to dampen when I ask about him getting a place to live.

"You should still take my mother's money. She feels bad keeping it." I dig into my purse and shove the wad of bills into his hand.

"No, honestly." He walks alongside me. "But if you insist, I'll hail you a cab. I'm sure you had a long day at work. You look tired."

I stare at the money, regretting it if he's going to waste it on a cab. I can't afford taxis. I don't even have a car since I borrow my mom's. But before I can say anything, Tyler waves one over. I'm too tired to argue, and besides, my sore feet appreciate it.

He opens the door for me and helps me into the backseat, then slides in next to me. After asking me where I'm headed, he gives the driver my mother's address.

Once we're on our way, he loops his arm over my shoulder and pulls me close to him. I hope he doesn't smell the pine cleaner on me. That would be so unromantic.

"Depending on traffic, we'll have some time to talk," Tyler says. "I'd like to see you again, but I'm worried about Bree, and I don't want her to get hurt if things don't work out between us."

Score one for honesty. He took the words right out of my mouth.

"I feel the same way. I'm hoping this father thing is a phase she'll grow out of."

He runs his fingers under my bandana and loosens it, letting my hair down. "That's better. As for Bree, do you mind telling me what the situation with her father is? I don't want to presume."

"She doesn't have one. I mean, biologically, of course she does, but I don't know who he is."

Tyler's breath draws in sharply. "You don't?"

"That came out wrong. I had artificial insemination."

"But why?" He blinks and turns to stare at my face. "I'm sure you had boyfriends."

"Not the same as someone you'd trust with a child. Maybe I was selfish, but I was very busy with work and had no time to date. Not that any of the men around me were prizes."

"Well, I'm glad." Tyler kisses the side of my temple. "Because I have a chance to be a prize catch for you."

I shake my head and chuckle. "Arrogant, aren't you? You get a job and now you're a catch?"

"Not as good a catch as you. Can I tell you I'm attracted to you?"

"Even in these clothes?"

"Well, maybe not." He quirks his eyebrows. "Better without clothes."

"Tyler Manning." I tap his chest. "I can't believe you just said that."

He catches my hand and kisses it. "Make a wish. Your luck is about to change."

"Am I supposed to tell you?" A fit of giggles hit me, and I squirm in his arms. I mean, there's the proper wish for world peace, and the practical one, me getting a better job, and then there's the hunk with his arms around me, smelling like Le Male cologne, powerful, masculine, and terribly sexy.

"Of course. I'm Father Christmas. Tell me, dear girl, what you want for Christmas."

"Sssh." I motion toward the cab driver, whose eyes glance at me from the mirror.

Tyler's breath is in my ear. "Deep in your heart, what do you really want for Christmas?"

You. Like that song says.

"A job using my skills and talents."

"Ahhh ... That's all?" He mocks disappointment, slowly shaking his head and frowning, one hand rubbing down the side of his face. "I don't think that's what you really want. But, you're in luck. The charity I got a job with is looking for an assistant to their chief financial officer. You can give me your résumé, and I'll hand it to them. Where did you say you used to work?"

I pull back from his side and fold my hands in my lap. "Actually, I'm not sure I should apply."

"Why not? If you worked on Wall Street, you're overqualified for the position. I'm sure you'll get it."

My pulse freezes. "Who told you I worked on Wall Street?"

"Bree. Only she thinks it's Wall-E Street where there are robots who collect trash."

"Oh, really? What else did she tell you?" I lighten my voice to a flirtatious chirp so he won't suspect I'm hiding anything.

"She talked about Central Park, the Macy's parade, and your sister mentioned you used to take her to FAO Schwarz."

"I thought she was too young to notice the difference. Now you know why I want her to have a perfect Christmas. Tree, presents, even ice skating like we did back in New York."

He rubs my arm. "I understand too well. Christmas used to be special for me when my father lived, but after he died, we didn't celebrate it anymore."

"That's so sad. Tyler, I didn't know." I reach for him and tuck my hand in his.

"I used to be bitter watching others celebrate Christmas, but since meeting you and Bree, and trimming the tree with your family, I changed my mind. I also want this to be your best Christmas ever, even better than when you had the Tiffany's tree."

I snuggle into his hunky chest and inhale his stimulating scent. "*Our* best Christmas ever."

Chapter 15

~ Kelly ~

I STEP OUT OF THE cab while Tyler pays the driver.

"Thanks for the ride." I kiss his cheek. "I think it's better if you don't come up because Bree will get overly excited."

"I was thinking the same thing. I'd hate for her to expect too much."

My lips move to Tyler's lips, and I speak into his mouth. "I still want to see you."

"That can be accomplished. San Francisco's a big city to get lost in. I'll take you anywhere you want to go."

His lips slide over mine, and I open my mouth, welcoming his deep kiss. If only things were simpler. If only I'd met Tyler before I screwed up and my life fell apart.

"See you tomorrow night?" he asks when we break to take a breath.

"Yes, tomorrow's my day off."

"Can't wait. I can't stop thinking about you, Kelly." His hands sweep down my side, and he holds my waist, pulling me close. "I want to be the man you dream about, the one you want and need."

Wow. What a difference a job makes. I like it. He's confident, earnest, aggressive. His erection stiffens against my belly, and instead of pulling away, I surprise myself by wiggling against him.

His lips return and lock onto mine, then his hands rove around from my waist, brushing the sides of my breasts. I slip my hands under his jacket, untucking his shirt, as a rush of desire slams me. His skin is hot over hard, firm muscles.

My belly tightens and heat curls between my legs. I want him so badly. Not any man, but Tyler. I gasp at the intensity of my emotions. I can't believe I'm about to undress him outside of my mother's apartment.

Tyler backs off, his eyes narrowed. "I'm sorry I got carried away. You're not upset, are you?"

I catch my breath, trying to inhale deeply. "I'm fine. Just tired. You won't believe how many bathrooms I cleaned. I feel grungy."

I'm glad for the darkening evening and the fact that we're in the shadows of my mother's building. He can't see the trembling of my lips, the sweat over my brow, my flushed cheeks. It isn't like me to get so horny, so turned on. I'm the sensible, responsible type. I have a daughter.

He tucks his shirt back into his pants. "How about dinner tomorrow evening?"

"Yes. Tomorrow, I'll see you tomorrow." I wave and retreat behind the gate.

"How will I contact you? Shall I come here?"

"No, I'll text Sawyer my address. I really have to go."

I have to sing at church tonight. And pray. Lots of prayer.

~ Tyler ~

Tyler's heart beat against his ribcage and sweat dampened his forehead. He and Kelly had met at her apartment, and he'd let her select the restaurant. This was it, his first date with her, and he couldn't screw it up. He took a deep breath as they crossed the street.

The tattered black, red, and green Afghan flag flapped in the wind against the gray, evening sky over Little Kabul. The tiny restaurant was sandwiched between two larger buildings. Its pockmarked sandstone colored walls and rusty gate seemed out of place among the festive, modern décor of the surrounding eateries.

"Ever been here before?" Kelly pushed her way through the creaky gate into a small, vine-covered courtyard. A mural of snow-covered mountains overlooked the entrance.

"First time." Tyler gripped Kelly's hand and steeled himself. The piquant fragrance of Afghan food mixed with gunpowder, dust, and smoke in his mind. But he forced himself to relax.

If he wanted to return to Afghanistan to do humanitarian work, he needed to get over the negative associations and replace them with positive emotions. At least that was what his therapist said.

They stepped through an ornate studded door and were greeted by a young woman wearing jeans, her hair tied back in a ponytail. No burka, no hijab.

"Smells just like barbeque," Kelly said after they were seated.

"Yep, nothing like roasted meat." Except when it was mixed with the scent of blood and peppered with the screams of grown men.

Tyler took another cleansing breath. He had to get these morbid thoughts out of his mind. He'd seated himself where he had a clear view of the door from one side and the open kitchen with the large grill on the other.

"Would you like to order drinks?" the waitress asked.

"I'll have the *doogh*," Kelly replied. "You should try it too."

"Yogurt and cucumbers?" He read the description on the menu.

"It's addictive, I'm telling you," Kelly said.

"Really good with kebobs," the waitress added.

"Okay, I'm game." He couldn't believe throughout his time in Afghanistan, he'd never sampled the street food, never been to a residence, never explored. Of course there were those rules of engagement. They'd been forbidden to mingle with the civilians, especially the women. So they'd stuck to their regiments, eating at the chow tent.

"Their kebobs are the best." Kelly pointed to the photos of reddish, charbroiled meat. "I usually get the lamb and *chaplee*. I'm a real meat eater."

"I'm surprised. I thought everyone here is vegan or organic."

"We have vegetarian entrees, too," the waitress said. "Roasted eggplant or squash."

"I'll have what she's having. How's the *chaplee*?"

"Spicy," the waitress said. "It's sort like a hamburger, except it has green onions, garlic, cumin and coriander mixed in."

"Sounds good." Tyler handed the menu to the waitress.

"How are you feeling?" Kelly asked after the waitress departed.

"Fine. It's just a restaurant."

"Yeah, but it's bringing back all sorts of memories, and I bet not all of them good."

"Can't blame an entire nation of people." Tyler shrugged. "They really decorated this place well."

One section had the traditional on-the-floor tables and cushions. A large mural depicting wild horses hung behind them across from another one showing travelers against the backdrop of shadowy mountains and high passes. The walls, however, were dark, blood-colored red, in contrast to the glazed blue pottery Afghanistan was famous for.

Kelly took his hand and rubbed it. Tension seeped out of Tyler's veins, replaced by warmth.

"Thanks, I'm really okay."

"I know you are. Don't think about the war. Think about the rebuilding, the reconstruction, the hope for a better future."

"That's what Warspring is all about." He switched tack. "That's the charity I'm working for. They accepted my proposal to set up sports programs for Afghan orphans."

"Really? That's awesome."

The waitress returned with their drinks. "I also brought you an appetizer, *pakawra*. I hate to call it Afghan French fries, because it's nothing like it, except it's a fried potato wedge, but really good."

The dark-orange colored wedges were huge, longer than a pickle and flattened.

The two women watched Tyler try the *pakawra*. It was slightly spicy, tasting like a large chili fry.

"Like it?" Kelly asked. "It's better if you dip it into the cilantro yogurt chutney."

"It's all good," Tyler said. The minty yogurt drink, *doogh*, reminded him of a sour, salty margarita without tequila. He could see why it was addictive.

There was nothing like food and a beautiful woman to pave over the fear warring in his gut. By the time the kebobs arrived, Tyler was able to breathe easy. Kelly's quiet and easy company was a wonderful gift, something he could hardly dare to wish for.

Add to that, her laughter and the way her honey-colored hair was highlighted against the soft lighting reignited a primitive instinct of desire and want. What could be better than a woman's comforting touch? Not just any woman, but Kelly Kennedy, someone with a head on her shoulders, able to empathize, having had enough life experiences to not be dismissive of his.

He clamped down his lustful imagination and steered them to more practical matters, like helping her get her wish for a better paying job.

"Have you thought about applying for the financial assistant position with Warspring?" he asked as the waitress refilled their drinks.

"I'm not sure I can." She wiped her lips, leaving lipstick on the napkin.

"Why not? You haven't been out of work long. Right? You were still working in New York last Christmas, less than a year ago."

"Sure, but a lot has happened since then." Kelly dipped a piece of flatbread in the yogurt sauce. "Let's not talk about it."

"Fair enough. I won't mention it, but here's Carina's contact. She's waiting for an email from you." He pushed the Warsping finance director's business card at her.

"Why, Tyler? Have you become my mother?" Kelly rolled her eyes and winked.

Oops. He didn't mean to come off pushy. He perused the dessert menu. "Any room for dessert?"

"Oh, no, I'm too stuffed. Why don't we take something home?"

He liked the sound of that. After ordering a *baklava* pastry and *firni*, a milk pudding topped with ground pistachios and a rosewater syrup, he paid the tab.

Fog had descended on the city by the time they walked out of Little Kabul. The wind had died and the frayed, stringy flag hung limp.

Tyler and Kelly meandered arm in arm down blocks of colorful row homes, every one stuck to its neighbor, but distinct in architecture and style.

They stepped through an alley and down the stairs around a dumpster. Kelly's apartment was tucked behind a low wall. She unlocked the flimsy hook of the screen door, but didn't slide the door to invite him in.

"I had a wonderful time," she said. "I hope you did too."

"I did." He placed his hands on her shoulders. "Can't beat the food and company. Want to do it again?"

"Sure." Her hazel-colored eyes darkened, and she bit her lips.

Something was off. Ever since he'd mentioned the job, she'd gone from open posture to closed. He wasn't going to get lucky tonight.

Might as well lean in for the kiss and cut his losses. Her mouth opened to say something, but Tyler swooped down and kissed her.

She tasted both spicy and sweet, honeyed like the baklava they'd nibbled during the walk to her place.

Tyler broke the kiss before Kelly. "I have to work tomorrow. What does your schedule look like?"

"Working every evening until Friday."

"Want to spend it with me or do you have something planned with your family?"

"Both. Bree's in a Christmas play at church."

"Great. What's she playing?"

"A sheep in the meadow." Kelly laughed. "But it's a big role for her. You won't believe how she rehearses her part. Baaa ... Baaa ..."

"Am I invited? Do you think it'll be okay if I show up?"

"Maybe, but it might be best if you weren't seen with the family."

"I understand." Tyler couldn't help his throat from tightening.

"Hey, but there's no reason why you and I can't have dinner beforehand. My mother can bring Bree to church." She tapped his chest and smiled. "You're so cute when you pout."

"I didn't pout."

"Did too." She reached up and kissed his cheek. "Dinner, my treat."

"Dinner it is, but I'm paying." Tyler caressed her shoulder. "I'm the man."

"I'm a woman who doesn't need a man." Kelly slid the glass door aside.

"Oh, I bet you have needs you're not even aware of."

"None that I can't take care of myself." Her heaving chest and the blush burning her face gave away what she was thinking.

"Ah, but the pleasure of the unexpected touch is a gift, not a command." He lowered his head and brushed his lips on her neck, kissing her pulse points and nibbling her skin.

She sucked in a sharp breath and melted against him. He made his way to her ear and nuzzled the lobe delicately. She quivered and a small moan escaped her throat.

“I’ll see you Friday,” he whispered. “Unless something comes up this week and you need my unexpected touch.”

Without waiting for her reply, he retreated into the fog.

Chapter 16

~ Kelly ~

"I'M GOING TO DO IT," I tell Mama. "This is a non-profit, so I don't think I'm violating my probation terms."

"I'd be careful." She looks over my shoulder at my laptop screen. "You're a convicted felon. You can't vote and you can't serve on a jury. Did you check with your probation officer?"

"They said it was okay for me to volunteer at Bree's school. This shouldn't be any different." I flick to the "About" page on Warspring's website. "See? It's a registered charity."

"What if they do a background check?" Mama pops a waffle into the toaster for Bree's breakfast.

"They hired Tyler on the spot. No background check. Tyler says Dave Jewell has a soft spot for those who are down and out. He's always taking food baskets to the homeless."

"Then go for it." She turns toward the hallway. "Bree. Wake up, honey. Today's a school day."

While she dresses Bree, I update my résumé, taking care to erase my last position in investment banking. What I have before then is sufficient. Intern, a finance degree, even the post-graduate analyst job with a different firm. If they ask me what I was doing for the last four years, it's simple. I had Bree, and I lived off my savings to give her a stay-at-home parent.

I hit 'send,' fish the waffles from the toaster, and check my inbox. There's a message from tyler@warspring.com already.

Tyler: *Carina says you applied. You free for lunch?*

Typical guy. Stringing on two thoughts in one note.

Me: *Sure, but maybe I should practice interviewing.*

I pour a glass of water for my mother and coffee for myself. My laptop rings with incoming email notifications.

Carina: *Can you come by today? Is eleven good?*

Tyler again: *They want to talk to you.*

Me to Tyler: *Oh, gosh. I don't know what to wear.*

Me to Carina: *Yes. Definitely.*

Tyler: *Don't dress too conservatively. Dylan's a real Bohemian.*

Carina: *Great. Directions attached.*

Me to Tyler: *But what about Carina? Let me google her.*

Tyler: *Not to worry. They're both really nice. Young too. Carina doesn't look like she's out of high school.*

Me to Carina: *Got it. Will be there.*

I step away from the laptop. "Mom, I got the interview. Today at eleven."

She peeks her head from the hallway. "That's great. But Bree's feeling hot. I don't think she can go to preschool today."

I rush to the room where Bree stays. My poor baby, between my cleaning job and date with Tyler, I've neglected her.

"Mama, I hot." Bree puts her hand over her forehead. "I wanna go school."

"Not when you're hot. Anything hurt?"

Bree points to her throat. "Owie."

"You'll have to stay home."

"But I wanna go. They have reindeer play today."

"She can stay here," Mama says. "I can cancel my appointment."

"No, it's important. I'll postpone the interview. I'm sure they'll understand. Bree, you want apple juice?"

The cold juice could help her throat. I go to the kitchen and pour a cup for her. She grabs it and climbs onto a chair to eat her waffle with honey.

The emails are still coming in. After giving Bree the juice, I stop by my laptop.

Tyler: *Think we can have lunch after the interview?*

Me: *Actually I have to postpone. Bree has a fever.*

Tyler: *Oh, bummer. Carina's schedule is booked solid until Friday, then she's taking off for the East Coast for the holidays. I can keep an eye on Bree for you. Is she too sick to come to the office?*

"I wanna go school." Bree pouts. "They have real reindeer. They pwo-mised."

Me: *A little sore throat. She wants to go to school. Should I stuff her with Tylenol and send her?*

Tyler: *No, she might expose the other kids and once the medicine wears off, she'll feel miserable. Bring her by. I'll take her for a walk or show her some of the toys Dylan collected from his travels.*

One thing's for sure. Tyler can be very persuasive.

Mama glances over my shoulder, reading my mail. "You should go. If you wait until after the holidays they might have found someone else. Who knows if Carina meets one of her old schoolmates while back home? I'll watch Bree."

"Mama, you're fasting for your appointment. It's bad enough I can't take you."

"I can still drive, you know. I'm not that old." Mother whispers, "Do you think it's wise for Tyler to watch Bree?"

"He won't hurt her."

"I know that," Mother says. "I'm thinking more about the father for Christmas thing."

"Oh, you're right. But I have a good feeling about him. We had a wonderful time last night."

"I know you did."

"He didn't even try to come into my apartment. He knew Bree was spending the night with you, but he held himself back. And he's really gung ho about me getting the job."

"That way he can see more of you." Mother winks. "Let me call Ella and see if she can watch Bree."

I slap myself on the forehead. Of course, Ella is on school break. "What's wrong with me? I almost went back on our agreement to have Tyler stay away from Bree."

"That's because you're falling for him, dear."

"It's too soon. I barely know him. I don't have time. If I get this job, I'll be busy."

"Not too busy for an office romance." Mother gives me an encouraging smile. "You deserve happiness. Don't you think you've paid enough already? The worst day of my life wasn't the day I found out I had cancer, it was the day you went to Riker's Island."

"Oh, Mom." I hug her. "Thanks for standing by me the entire time, even though I wasn't with you for your treatments."

"Hush, your heart was in the right place. I know you did it for the experimental treatment we couldn't afford."

"It's no excuse though. No excuse."

~ Tyler ~

"May I see you in my office a moment?" Carina stood outside of Tyler's cubicle. He had finished confirming the speakers for the Donor's Ball coming up this Friday.

"Sure, I was wondering if I could have an extra ticket to the ball. I promised a friend of mine, another veteran, to be my guest, but I wonder if Kelly can also get an invite."

Carina's eyebrows turned down, and her nose scrunched, as if smelling trouble. "Actually that's what I wanted to talk to you about."

Alarm bells jangled in Tyler's mind, and sweat prickled his skin. He walked the few steps to Carina's office.

She shut the door and pointed to her monitor. "Have you seen this?"

"Uh, no." He craned his neck to look over her shoulder. "Who's that? Kelly? Can't be. She's a single mother who works in a cleaning service."

The headline read, "Wall Street Director Convicted of Insider Trading."

"It's Kelly all right." She brought up another page with her mug shot and read, "Kelly Kennedy of Goldfinch Securities has been sentenced to three months in Federal Prison on securities violations and insider trading. Leniency was given in this case because of the perpetrator's young daughter and elderly mother suffering from cancer, and the fact that Kennedy did not profit from the trade. She lost all her assets totaling ..."

"I didn't know. Honestly." Tyler sagged into a chair and ran his hands up and down his pants legs.

"How long have you known her?" Carina handed him a printout. "She lied on her résumé. Look at this. 'Time out to be a stay-at-home mother for my daughter.' We can't hire her."

"I had no idea."

"Let me send her an email cancelling." Carina glanced at her watch. "Now I can meet Dylan at The Brewed Force across the Bay. He's auditioning for a guitar player since he hurt his wrist."

"The Brewed Force, where's that?"

"Berkeley." Carina's lips quirked. "You're really a caveman, aren't you? Everything's on the internet these days. I'll ask Dylan to pick you up a smartphone."

"Sure thing."

"No problem." Carina squeezed his arm. "Too bad your friend didn't work out. I printed you an extra ticket. Just keep Kelly away from Dylan's father and his friends. Now that I think about it, haven't you ever wondered why she's a maid at Mogul Bank? She's probably going through the wastebaskets or eavesdropping. The question is, whose side is she on? The government or her cronies?"

Tyler squeezed his fists inside his pockets. He wasn't about to speculate or contradict Carina. "Thank you for the tickets. I'll prepare the speaker's folders and have them on your desk by tonight."

"Great. Lock up. I won't be back until late. Dylan's sure to take all day." She picked up her suit jacket and purse and gave him a stiff smile. "Try not to blame yourself. You didn't know. Next time, make it your business to know everything about everyone who contacts Warspring. Our reputation is all that we have as far as donors are concerned."

"Yes, ma'am." Tyler wiped the sweat from his brow and turned to his work after sending Sawyer an email about the audition.

As for Kelly, he was through with her. He should have trusted his instincts and not pushed her to apply for the job. It was obvious she'd been hiding something, although truth to tell, he thought it was Bree's father. He hadn't believed her artificial insemination story.

But insider trading? Wall Street greed? Bailouts? Fraud? Junk securities foisted on unsuspecting pension plans? Wiping out honest people's savings? Kelly had been a part of it. Not just a part, but she'd hoped to profit by cheating.

How well did he know her? Apparently not well enough. The façade she played at her church was just that: the efficient volunteer, the careful mother, the independent woman. How much was real? She'd only expressed real interest in him after he'd gotten the job at Warspring. Had she been planning on using him to bilk Warspring?

He was still creating the handouts when someone rang the buzzer. The receptionist was out, so Tyler answered it.

"Kelly." He startled at the sight of her and sucked in a breath. She was stunning, more stunning than her friend, the redhead, looking every bit the investment banker from her well-tailored suit jacket to the tips of her shiny black leather pumps.

"Am I late?" Kelly glanced over his shoulder at the clock.

"No, you didn't get Carina's email?"

She stepped in after him. "I last checked before getting on the train. Why? Did she have to go somewhere?"

"Oh, that's right. You don't have a smartphone." Tyler rocked on the balls of his feet. "You can login from my computer, or I can boot up the receptionist's."

He reached under the desk and turned it on. "I have to finish the speaker's materials. I'll be right over there."

"Tyler?" Kelly placed a hand on his arm. "You won't even look at me. You know, don't you?"

"Yes, I know, and so does Carina." He jerked himself away from her. He'd seen his family and neighbors lose their homes and farms, and had their small businesses swallowed up by vulture capitalists.

Kelly followed him to his cubicle. "I can explain."

"I don't want to hear it. I'm busy."

"I understand." She lowered her face and turned toward the door. "All I wanted was a chance, a second chance."

Tyler's throat was dry, his mouth frozen, but he didn't stop her from walking out the door.

Chapter 17

~ Kelly ~

"HEY, YOU'RE BACK EARLY." ELLA glances from the couch and switches off the TV. "Bree's doing better. She's a little sleepyhead, but she ate lunch and drank lots of fluids. How did the interview go?"

"It was over before it even started." I kick off my uncomfortable but stylish heels. "They knew."

"Crap. What about Tyler? What did he say?"

"He doesn't want to have anything to do with me." I recount his attitude, how he couldn't even speak two kind words to me.

"He doesn't know why you did it. How desperate we all were with Mother's apartment in foreclosure, and her insurance company upping the premiums."

"It doesn't matter. I broke the law. Thanks for watching Bree."

"I thought he was into you. I can't believe he didn't listen." Ella follows me to Mother's bedroom where I'd left my street clothes.

"I don't need him anyway. It's all for the best. At least Bree won't get hurt." I blink and turn toward the wall.

"Do you think he'll still come to Bree's Christmas play?"

"I doubt it." I unbutton my linen shirt and hang it. "I saw tickets on the printer for the Annual Donor's Ball for Friday. One of them had my name on it and another one had Sawyer McGee, Tyler's friend who busks in the subway."

"That's good, isn't it? He was planning to invite you."

I unzip my skirt. "Was. Did he think I'd miss Bree's play for his fancy ball? Doesn't matter now. He didn't invite me."

"That sucks." Ella crosses her arms and juts her jaw. "Really sucks. If I ever see Tyler, I'm going to give him a piece of my mind. Arrogant wuss."

It's always heartwarming to have family stick up for me. I reach over and grab my sister for a hug. She might have her quirks and lives in a world of dance and costumes, but she's always had my back, even though she's more than ten years younger than me.

"Don't worry about it. Bree and I will be just fine without Tyler."

"Is Ty coming to Chwistmas play?" Bree's little voice pipes from the doorway.

I throw on a t-shirt and pick her up, pressing a hand on her forehead. "You feeling better, honey? You're not as hot."

"Me not hot. Yay!" Bree puts both hands up in the air like she crossed the finish line at a race. "I want Ty to play reindeer with me. He can let me ride on his back. I tie a string on his nose and pull."

"Ty's busy. Maybe Jaden can do the reindeer for you," I say, darting a glance at Ella.

"Yes, Jaden's a funny reindeer. He can jump and prance all the way up the chimney." Ella pantomimes reindeer prancing on the rooftop.

Bree claps her hands. "You marry Jaden and Mommy marry Ty. I be flower girl."

"Whee!" Ella takes Bree from me and spins her around. "Want to put on that daisy costume I made for you? I'll be the ladybug and you can be a flower."

"Will Mommy be the bumblebee?"

"Yes, perfect!" Ella squeals.

"Oh, no, if I bad girl, Mommy sting me."

"She won't. Bees love flowers because they make honey from flowers." Ella flows a kiss on Bree's cheeks.

She's good at distraction. I finish changing and hang my clothes in the dry cleaning bag. I won't be needing business outfits at the rate things are going. My cleaning shift starts in a few hours so I better start cooking dinner.

~ *Tyler* ~

Tyler completed his tasks early. After updating all the slides, he printed and collated the handouts and assembled the folders. It was a little after five, and he still had time to catch Kelly before her six to midnight shift at Mogul.

He shouldn't have let her walk out without giving her a chance. Hadn't she given him a chance when she trusted him with Bree after knocking her down? She'd even allowed him to take her to the park and hang out with her family.

A dull ache sat in his belly at the way he'd dismissed her, as if she were nothing but a common criminal. During his break, he'd searched the internet. Her mother had been at death's door and her apartment was being foreclosed on. Her friend, Rebecca Morley, had raised money for Kelly's legal fees. The website was still up. Not that it was right or moral, but Kelly had wanted to pay for her mother's costly treatments.

She'd been remorseful and earned a light sentence. Shouldn't he, of all people, allow her a chance to explain? Besides, when Kelly walked out, it was like a piece of him left with her, leaving him hollow and achy.

He stopped by a florist and bought a bouquet of gardenias and lilies, adding a giant candy cane to his purchase.

~ *Kelly* ~

Donna, the receptionist, hangs up the phone and wags her eyebrows. "He's been here again."

A bouquet of roses, larger than yesterday's orchids, sits on the front desk of Mogul Bank.

"You keep them."

Donna makes a sad pouty face. "He's not interested in me. Why would I want his flowers?"

"I don't know. Donate them? I can't eat or gift them."

"Whatever happened, he's awfully sorry," Donna says, handing me a golden box of chocolates. "Let's see, Monday was the gardenias and lilies with the jumbo candy cane, Tuesday, assorted tulips and giant lollipop, yesterday orchids and chocolate dipped strawberries, and now we've graduated to red roses. You know what they say about red roses and a box of Godiva chocolates. L. O. V. E."

"It's nothing like that. I gotta get to my job." I keep the chocolates and take one last look at the array of flowers, my heart aching at the emptiness of the gesture. He feels guilty, nothing else.

I slave over the kitchens and bathrooms, wiping up a conference room with more spills and splats than an elementary school cafeteria. Must have been some food fight.

By midnight, I'm exhausted. The day off tomorrow is a godsend. I tuck the box of chocolates under my arm and exit the building. Bree's been sleeping over at Mother's all week because Ella's home from college and plays with her all day.

I exit the building and head for the BART. The last train departs in less than half an hour so I have to hurry.

"Kelly." Tyler jogs up to me. "Can we talk?"

He's wearing his old raincoat, a pair of holey jeans, a sweatshirt, and a watch cap. He presents a single red rose, probably plucked from the bouquet he knew I wasn't going to keep.

"Not now. I'm running late." I avoid facing him and keep walking.

"I shouldn't have treated you the way I did."

"Why not? I'm a convicted felon." My voice is hard and clipped.

"You paid your penalty. I'm sure jail was unpleasant."

"Look, if it makes you feel better, thanks for the candy. Bree and my mother enjoyed them, although I didn't tell them who donated them." I increase my speed to a jog.

"Kelly, don't cut me off."

"I'm not, but if I don't make that train, I'll miss the connecting bus and I'll have to walk the rest of the way home."

He grabs my arm. "I'll call a cab."

"I'm not riding in a cab with you, and I can't afford the fare. You know that. Not many employers will take a chance with a jailbird."

He punches something on a new smartphone. "Stay still. A car's coming."

"Take the chocolate." I shove the golden box into his hands and sprint toward the train station.

"Kelly." He gives chase and runs me down within a block, grabbing my arm. "Give me a chance. Everyone deserves a second chance. Don't I?"

A car honks and a yellow cab pulls to the curb. Tyler opens the door. What choice do I have? At the rate he keeps stopping me, I'll miss public transportation.

I slide into the back seat, and he gets in after me. He doesn't attempt to speak to me, preferring to chat up the driver, an Ethiopian man who used to be a college professor.

We arrive at my apartment. Tyler pays the fare. Silently, I walk to my unit with him glued to my side.

"Don't you have to work tomorrow?" I ask when I open my sliding glass door.

"They gave me the day off in light of the Donor's Ball. I got a ticket for you."

I step into my apartment and turn on the light. "Sorry, can't go. Bree's play, remember?"

"You must be really tired." He puts a warm hand on my shoulder. "Her play is Saturday night. I checked the church website."

"Are you sure?"

He shows me the screen on his smartphone. Sure enough, I had the date wrong.

"I'm still not going to the ball with you. I'm sure I won't be welcome. They'd think I was there to steal from them."

He grabs me be the arms. "Stop it. Stop cutting yourself down."

"I'm only speaking the truth. What changed? Did you read up about me? What my friends said? What my family was going through? What jail was like for me? How they abused me because I was the Gucci girl? The rich white bitch? The guards would randomly announce a search, dump out our mattresses and make us strip naked and squat in front of them, like we're hiding knives in our private parts. Humiliated, degraded, and humbled. Is that why you're here?"

"No." His grip tightens. "I'm here because I care about you. I want to help you."

"Sorry." I peel his hands from me. "I'm not your project."

He grabs both sides of my cheeks and lowers his head until we're nose to nose. "I want you, Kelly, as a woman."

Sparks fly and my resistance short circuits behind the tide of wanting and needing. His lips meet mine, fitting perfectly. Sensations I've never felt before bloom over my body, everything coming alive.

His lips and tongue speak to my very soul, comforting and exciting. He backs me until my legs touch the sofa. I float down onto the cushions. Tyler sheds his raincoat onto the floor and kneels at the side of the couch.

Our lips reconnect. There's an urgency, a hunger that wasn't there before. He slides over me, propping himself with his elbows, his knees still on the floor.

He smells rough, like he'd been out in the sun, unlike the smooth banker fragrance he wore earlier. My hands sneak under his sweatshirt. Our lips part as I pull the shirt over his head, then rejoin after a gasp of air.

I drag my hands over his chest, the light sprinkling of hair in the center, then trace the intricate dragon tattoo over his shoulder and down his back.

He removes his black watch cap, and his hair falls onto my forehead. We continue to kiss, growing hungrier with each stroke, each smack.

I'm hot and want to remove my sweatshirt. Pausing to pull it up, I interrupt the kiss. Instead of helping me, Tyler's body tenses and he pushes away from me. I toss my shirt, but it's too late.

He gets off the floor and stands. "I came to talk to you, not to seduce you."

Shame engulfs me, heating my skin red hot. I close my eyes and lay back. Nervous laughter jiggles my belly. "I'm tired. I can't go on like this."

"If you want to sleep, I'll stay here on the couch." His voice is gentle, comforting. "We can talk in the morning."

"That sounds good. I'm going to take a shower." I lift myself from the sofa and pull a blanket from the linen closet. "Will this be warm enough?"

"For a guy who sleeps on the street, this is a 5-star hotel." He shakes the blanket over the sofa. "Good night. Thanks for letting me stay."

Chapter 18

~ Kelly ~

A MAN'S CHOKED SCREAM WAKES me. I sit up in my bed, my heart racing. It's silent. Did I dream it? I turn over and rest my head on the pillow. My pulse swishes in my ear. There it is again. A garbled cry. Tyler.

Rushing into the living room, I find him on the floor, his eyes wide open staring at the ceiling. He's thrown the blanket.

"Tyler." I kneel and reach for him.

"Stay back." He blocks my progress. His breathing is rapid and shallow, and sweat runs down his forehead, plastering his blond curls to his temples.

"Tyler, I'm here." I maneuver myself into his field of vision.

Gradually the blank stare gives way to recognition and his breathing slows. His jaw slackens and he whispers, "Kelly."

His eyes twitch and close. He sucks in several loud breaths, shuddering in between, but he seems calmer.

I brush the hair from his face and kiss his cheek. "Are you okay?"

He doesn't answer. His chest rises and falls steadily, as if he's fallen back asleep. Taking a wet paper towel, I wipe the sweat from his face, then blow.

"That feels good," he murmurs.

"You're awake?"

He doesn't answer, but when I pull his hand and tell him to get up, he complies. I lead him to my bed and pull him in with me.

He sighs and relaxes as soon as he hits the mattress. "I need you."

"Stay here with me." I rest my head on his chest and he wraps his arms around me. "I don't want to be alone anymore."

"Me either." He kisses the top of my head.

I yawn and close my eyes, lulled by his steady, strong heart. Every thump speaks of another chance, another tomorrow, a future, and maybe, just maybe, a father for Bree.

When I wake, Tyler is already up. He wipes his wet hair with a towel. "I took a shower, I hope it's okay."

I allow my eyes to feast on him. It's more than okay. He's muscular, but not bulky. Water droplets glisten on his chest, and the tattoo running over his shoulder around his bicep sharpens his sexiness.

I swallow hard and lighten the mood. "Of course. I always bring guys home for a shower."

He chuckles, pulling on the towel to dry himself. "Did I scare you last night?"

"Come, sit here." I pat the bed. "You didn't scare me. You never do."

"I'm taking my meds, trying to keep everything in control." His weight lowers the mattress. "I'm really trying."

"So am I."

Trying to keep from jumping your bones.

I lower my gaze to his legs. "I'm not a criminal."

"You're not. I trust you." He rubs my shoulder, kneading away the tension.

A flurry of excitement spreads from his firm, strong hands. I almost purr at the sparks arcing between us. I can't let him know how he affects me. I'm not a weak woman.

Stiffening my back, I give him a push. "You're only saying that because you have nothing to steal. Try trusting me with the assets of your foundation."

"I'll speak to Dylan. He'll give you a chance."

"I don't deserve it. I lied to them." I swing my legs from the bed. "So, what are we going to do today?"

"Play hooky. Spend the day together, and go to the ball tonight. I'm sure you have a few clothes left." He lifts his jaw in an arrogant tilt, smirking.

Since when did I agree to go to the ball with him? Get the man a job and suddenly he's Prince Charming?

"Ever been bankrupt?" I head him off at the pass. "I had Ella clean out my closet before the court ordered inventory. They let you keep a few outfits and an old car, but Ella sold almost everything for Mother's medical bills."

Tyler takes my hand and drags me from the bed. "I don't care if you go to the ball looking like Cinderella. It wasn't long ago that I wore rags. As it is, I only have one suit."

"Then we're a matched pair." I laugh, picking up his sweatshirt and jeans and shoving them between us.

"So you'll go with me?"

"I suppose I should. Maybe I can make my own appeal to Dylan and Carina. I did some research. Did you know my friend Rebecca used to run the foundation, and she was the founder's best friend?"

"Oh, that should go well. Maybe she can speak for you." He wraps me into his arms and buries a kiss on the side of my neck. "Want breakfast in bed?"

What is he doing tempting me?

My knees wobble and heat swells in the pit of my belly. I close my eyes, but the visual of Tyler with a towel draped around his neck, his fiercely tattooed chest, and hair still dripping from the shower sends crashing waves of heat through my body.

"I want *you* in bed." My voice surprises me with its huskiness.

"About time you admitted it. You sure?"

I swallow my drool, ignoring his cockiness, and nod. Holding him last night, I had ample opportunity to explore the planes of his muscles and bones, snuggle on his chest. It's time to act.

Tyler glides over me, his muscles rippling against my sensitive skin. His mouth crashes over mine, more urgent and possessive than I expect. A moan drags from my throat. My mind blanks. All sensation stops except for everything Tyler: the press of his body, his fresh, wet scent straight from the shower, the pulsing sensations between our lips, the heated touch and currents of desire cresting lower down.

Just as I ease back into the bed, buried under the solid haven of Tyler's weight, a ringtone jangles from his new smartphone.

Tyler lifts his head, waits, then lowers his lips to my chest. The ringing stops, but starts again a few seconds later.

"It's probably my work," Tyler mumbles and backs off the bed. "Be right back."

He takes the phone to the living room.

I roll onto my tummy, still in a haze of desire, surrounded by his heat. How'd I get so lucky to find a man so honorable, kind, and brave? Sure, he has his issues, but he's accepted my past and he trusts me. Trusts me with his vulnerability.

Tyler returns with a scowl on his face. "I hate to do this to you, but Carina called. She wants me to change out the speakers' bios and add inspirational quotes."

My excitement at spending a day with Tyler flattens like road kill under an eighteen-wheeler. I pull my nightgown to cover my thighs. "Actually I should take Bree ice skating. She's feeling better, and it'll be a nice outing for us."

"You're still coming to the Donor's Ball with me this evening?"

"I'll think on it while I shower." I throw on a robe and brush by him on my way to the bathroom. The sampling of his taste and touch is enough to start my fantasies flowing. Forget a cold shower, I'm going for a long, hot, and stimulating one. By myself, unfortunately.

When I emerge from the shower, he's gone.

The faded red rose sits in a crystal bud vase beside a plate of toast and eggs and a glass of orange juice.

The invitation with my name is placed on the chair. I pick it up. He's scrawled a note: *Sorry I have to run. Be mine, Kelly. One night. Tonight. I have needs, too. Tyler.*

~ *Kelly* ~

"I want to ice skate." Bree holds my hand as we return to my mother's apartment. "I don't like the rain."

"We need rain, honey, for the plants and the trees."

"What if it's raining Chwistmas Eve? How's Santa gonna fly in the rain?"

We step through the door, and I remove her boots. "Santa can fly through a blizzard. A little rain isn't going to hurt."

"What about when I play the sheep with baby Jesus? I don't want sleep on wet hay."

"You'll be snuggly warm in your costume, and there's no rain on the stage."

"But if it rains, the stable might leak."

I give her a kiss and take off her jacket. "How about I make you a cup of hot cocoa?"

Ella holds her arms wide for a hug. "Bree, don't be such a little worrywart like your mother. Everything's great. Wanna dress up?"

"Yay!" Bree claps her hands. "Can I be a fairy princess?"

Together, Ella and Bree skip toward Mother's closet.

"Guess she's forgotten all about the skating." Mama helps me off with my coat and hangs it. "Tyler dropped by at lunchtime. Why aren't you picking up his calls?"

"It's too much pressure." I lower my face. "He wants me to try and get that job again. I lied on the application. There's no way they'll hire me."

"Then go as his guest and don't think about it. Did you call Rebecca and ask her to put in a good word for you?"

"I did. She thinks I shouldn't waste my time with Warspring. Since she's no longer at Mogul Bank, she said I can pass tips I hear in the hallways to her."

"But, that's illegal."

"I know. I turned her down. She got upset and asked if I was going to work for the government as a snitch. What should I do? Should I work in enforcement? They'll pay me well, although nothing close to banker salaries."

"It's up to you." Mother rubs the back of my neck. "You're stressed and tensed. Too busy worrying about the future to enjoy the present. You've got a decent, hunk of a man interested in you. Let's go through the closet and see what dresses Ella saved for you, and get you ready for the ball."

I turn around and kiss her cheek. "Thanks, fairy godmother. You're right."

"Text him right now. Tell him you'll be ready in an hour, no make that two."

"Will he still want me to attend?"

"Stop worrying," Mother says, then calls, "Ella, Bree, we're going to dress Cinder-Kelly up for the ball with Prince Charming."

"Yay," Ella and Bree squeal in unison and crowd around me.

Mother twirls her index finger like a wand. "One glass slipper coming up."

Chapter 19

~ Kelly ~

THE BANQUET EXCEEDS MY EXPECTATIONS: posh hotel, organic gourmet food, dancing and mingling, with a wine list to rival investment banking parties.

And Tyler. Wow is an understatement. Dressed in a tux with tails, with his athletic build and dark blond looks, he's the picture perfect spokesman for Warspring International. Unfortunately, it means I'm a tag-along as we're introduced to a dazzling array of important people: business leaders, CEOs, congress-people, and other high profile donors.

I'm in the powder room to freshen my makeup and pin the loose strands of my hair back. I straighten my evening gown with beaded accents designed to accentuate my curves and tuck a bra strap back in place.

Rebecca appears behind me.

She sets her clutch on the marble counter and plucks out her compact. "Have you given more thought to my offer? You're so talented, it doesn't seem right for you to be locked out of finance."

"It's okay. There are other avenues to explore."

"Seems you've caught yourself the man of the hour. Every woman out there's filling out pledge cards in astronomical amounts. All those funds will need to be invested."

"I'm sure Warspring has their fund managers."

"A twenty-one-year-old college dropout. She only got the job because she's sleeping with the founder's son."

"You mean Carina? I thought she was young."

"Still chewing with her milk teeth." Rebecca sniffs. "By the way, I'm still on the board. One word from me, and I can have you in place."

"But the probation?" My hand trembles as I reapply my mascara.

"We'll create a job for you. Receptionist or office assistant. Then you can monitor their investments on their internal computer system. I have a password you can use."

"I can't. If I get caught—"

"I'll pay for Bree's tuition to the most exclusive preschool, then private school. Would you prefer the French School or an alternative learning program?"

"You asked me how prison was."

"Money talks, even in jail." She lines her blood red lips.

"Yes, it does, but it's hell just the same." I snap my clutch shut. "You've helped me make my decision."

"What do you mean?" Her mouth forms a perfect O as she applies her lipstick.

"I'm going to take the offer with the Feds. Only fair to warn you, dear friend."

"Then I must warn you, dear friend. Mr. Manning's fair game for a quick roll in the penthouse." She plucks her clutch from the counter and steps to the bathroom door. "Good luck among all the fishes."

I wait thirty seconds before exiting the powder room. The conversation with Rebecca brings me back to the dog-eat-dog world of investment banking where everyone has a price tag and everything's for sale.

No more. When I walk back to the cocktail bar, I find Tyler surrounded by gorgeous socialites. His gaze locks onto mine. He excuses himself and makes a laser line toward me.

"How are you holding up?" He kisses me behind my ear. "Let me know when you want to leave."

"Party's just getting started. Want to dance?" I tug him toward the ballroom. "I'm waiting for you to sweep me off my feet."

"That can be accomplished, but first, let me wish Dylan and Carina a Merry Christmas. The office is shut next week for the holidays."

Hand in hand, we meander around the bar to the head table. The band on stage plays a bluesy tune, and couples are swaying to the rhythm.

I point to the guitar player. "Hey, isn't that Sawyer?"

"Yep," Tyler says. "He got the job. I overheard Dylan saying he was auditioning for a backup guitar player, and I sent him over."

"At least one of your referrals worked out."

"You want me to speak to Carina again?" He touches my shoulder, his fingers lightly caressing.

"No, I've decided to work with the Feds. Going to be a snitch."

"I'm proud of you." He sweeps his thumb across my chin. "You're one of the good guys now."

A man taps Tyler's shoulder. "Hate to interrupt, but my father wants to meet you."

Tyler's gaze lingers on me a moment longer before he replies, "Dylan, this is my date, Kelly Kennedy. Kelly, Dylan Jewell."

"Enchanted." Dylan takes my hand. "Let's meet my large family. Every one of us is delighted to have Tyler be the public face for Warspring."

Tyler rests his hand on the small of my back while Dylan leads me to the head table. A silver-haired man with piercing blue eyes looks up.

"That's my dad, Rich Jewell."

I stop short, causing Tyler to bump into me. Dylan's father has his arm around Rebecca.

"Dad, this is Tyler Manning and Kelly Kennedy."

I greet Mr. Jewell. If he remembers my notoriety, he makes no sign of it as he returns the cordialities.

Rebecca appears not to know me. She gives me a disinterested once over, then leers at Tyler. Funny, I never noticed her canines were so long.

"Rebecca Morley, my father's fiancée," Dylan continues with the introductions. "Tyler Manning and Kelly Kennedy."

"Enchanted," Rebecca speaks to the air between us. She then smothers Tyler with praise, asking him about Afghanistan and his tours of duty. Tyler tugs at his collar and rocks on his feet, clearly uncomfortable with her devouring attention. He turns me toward Carina.

She gives me a close-mouthed smile and dismisses me, not mentioning the interview or position, and then I'm introduced to Dylan's siblings: three brothers, Brad, Trent, and Crash, and two sisters, Kayla and Storm. Crash and Storm are teenaged twins, the babies of the family.

"That's a lot of Jewells," I say to Tyler when we're out of their earshot. "I can't believe Rebecca's in the middle of it. She doesn't seem to be the charitable type."

"You know her better than I do," Tyler says. "Should I watch my back?"

"Back, front, top, bottom, inside, out."

"Thanks for the warning." Tyler chuckles. "One more thing. They want to pay a tribute to their mother, Ava Jewell. Dylan asked me to pick the speaker. I hate to spring it on you, but would you say a few words about the importance of second chances, and why every orphan deserves a second chance, no matter their background or circumstance?"

"Sure, I'll be delighted." I straighten my posture as the familiar growl of adrenaline shoots through my veins, energizing me. I always loved the spotlight and the sheer power of being on top. How I missed it all this last year, humbled by my mistakes.

I breathe a silent prayer of gratitude to God and head for the podium.

~ *Kelly* ~

"You were awesome." Tyler kisses the tip of my nose.

I unlock the sliding glass door to my apartment and giggle. "Are you trying to talk your way in?"

"I don't know about you, but I'm getting out of the rain." He lets the umbrella down and shakes it.

"Poor homeless guy. Guess you'll have to take the couch again." I brush my body against his as we enter my apartment.

He drops his overnight bag on the floor. "I was hoping to get a spot at the foot of your bed."

I remove the goofy Santa hat the party goers made him wear. "Maybe if you're extra special nice, Mr. Claus."

"I think Mrs. Claus prefers naughty." His breath is hot in my ear, sending electric shivers over my body.

"Make that a shot of naughty and a lot of nice. Let's dance." I loosen his bowtie and wrap my hands around his neck, eager to feel the press of his majestic body against mine.

"Mmm, you're right. We can make up for it now." He slides his arms around me, pulling me close. "More private."

"Private, I like." I sway in his arms. The silence is broken only by the thumping raindrops, the swish of our breathing, and the beat of my love-crazed heart.

He asked for one night. A night for his needs, and I aim to give it to him. Waking up this morning with him and not touching him was pure torture. Last night had been about comfort. Tonight, much more.

I unbutton the top three buttons of his shirt and kiss his chest below the collarbone. The faint trace of earthy musk revs my pulse, thrumming moisture between my legs. "Make love to me, Tyler."

"I want to, wanted to since I laid eyes on you." He captures my mouth with a long, slow kiss while his hands stroke and explore my body.

Floods of desire crash over me, pent-up from a decade of withheld appetite. Nothing I've tasted or touched can compare to the sharp desperation of wanting Tyler, needing him, skin to skin, heart to heart, deep inside me. What started out slow and easy escalates rapidly, the kisses turning ravenous and grabbing.

Walking backward, I guide him into my bedroom while shedding his clothes. He runs his fingers over the beads on my gown and unzips it. I let it slip to the floor.

He sucks in a jagged breath as he turns me in his arms. "Wait. I don't have protection."

"Neither do I."

The look of consternation on his face would be comical if I weren't as equally disappointed.

"Guess I fail the Boy Scout test." He leans back and wipes his forehead. "I don't think we should take any chances."

Think? Who's thinking? Score one for responsible and vigilant.

"You can think of something. You're quite a handyman." I sag onto the bed and hold up my arms for him.

"You got it, your unexpected touch." He grins, before swooping over me and kissing me hard and deep, holding me tight and tender.

Everything inside of me responds to him, feeling safe, desired, and protected. Sweeping his hair from his face, I gaze into his warm, blue eyes. "I want you for more than a single night. Let me heal your wounds. Let me be the one to love you."

His mouth turns down and he closes his eyes, shaking his head. "I want you too, but you don't know what I did."

Chapter 20

~ Kelly ~

TYLER'S FACE IS STONY AND guarded. "I'll always have nightmares. I can't promise you I'll ever be healed. There are sights and sounds you'll never want to share."

I cling to his strong shoulders. "I want to help you. Don't you believe in second chances?"

"I'm a killer." His voice breaks. "There's no second chance for the dead."

"It was your job. It was kill or be killed."

He lowers his face and pinches the bridge of his nose. "I shot a child, Kelly. A child."

My entire body freezes, and the hairs stand up on the back of my neck. "How? When?"

Tyler's eyes glaze over with a faraway look. Sweat erupts on his face. His jaw shudders as his breath sizzles between his teeth.

"A boy about ten or eleven. He was crying, yelling, wearing a suicide vest. We could have disarmed him. We could have helped him."

I wrap my arms around Tyler, bringing his head onto my chest. "You had to stop him. He would have killed others."

"He was scared. He kept yelling and had his hand on a string attached to his vest. He was shaking from head to toe. I told him to stop."

I wipe the sweat off his brow, kissing the top of Tyler's head. "You saved more lives by shooting him."

"No, I didn't. The crowd gathered around him. Some were screaming in anguish and others yelling at me. A bunch of guys from my platoon were closer to him and went to break up the commotion. Then the boy blew up."

Tyler's entire body quakes, and his breathing is harsh. He scratches his face, his fingers digging into his flesh. His eyes squeeze shut. A heartrending cry shrieks from his mouth. "That kid never had a chance."

"You have to forgive yourself. It's not your fault."

His shoulders heave, and sobs hiccup from his throat. He smashes his fist into the bed, curling himself into a fetal posture, turning his back to me. "Leave me. Never come near me again."

I latch onto him from the back. "I'm not giving up on you. I swear to you, Tyler, I won't leave you."

"Why? I'm useless to you."

I can do nothing but hold onto him, using my body to press against him, to comfort him. What words are there? It wasn't his fault, but he doesn't believe it.

I rub his back, long strokes down his spine. I pepper him with kisses, tasting the salty tears. I press my cheek against his harsh stubble and hum the lullabies I use to put Bree to sleep.

My caresses loosen the tight knots of his shoulders and dissipate the stiffness in his neck. After a while, he calms, swallowing and taking deep breaths.

He closes his eyes, his lips moving as if in prayer. "I don't deserve forgiveness. Even if I spend the rest of my life helping the children, I can't bring that boy back. I can't bring anyone back."

"Do you believe in God? Do you believe He loves you?"

"I'm too screwed up for anyone to love me."

"That's not true. Ask God to forgive you. He'll hear you."

"I've already asked, but it's not enough. I have to do more."

"You're already giving all your money, and now you're going to start a program for them. What more can you do?"

A vein throbs in his temple and he takes my hand. "I have only one life to give, and I can't give it to you. I can't live a normal life, buy a house, raise a family, retire and travel."

It's a hard pill to swallow. But it's his life to give. I feel him slipping from my grasp, as if his memory is fading, and our love is already a bygone what-could-have-been.

I make one more pitch. "You're giving all to the orphans, but who's giving to you? Who'll make you happy and take care of your needs?"

"I can't ask you to make that sacrifice. You have Bree. She needs you, so does your mother." He cups my cheek and his eyes mist. "You made me very happy tonight. But after the holidays, I have a very busy fundraising schedule. Eventually I'll move to Afghanistan to run the sports camps."

"We still have Christmas Eve and Christmas together." I bite my lip, holding back the tears. "Spend it with me and my family."

"It's not fair to include me. I don't want to hurt any of you, especially Bree."

"She'll be fine. I'll tell her you're an angel sent to bless us this Christmas. Please, come to Bree's Christmas play. You'll make her very happy."

"Kelly." He kisses me on the forehead, his lips lingering. "It's easier if I leave now. You still have time before Christmas to spend with her. Take her last minute shopping, skating, go to the Nutcracker ballet."

"Don't leave me." Tears well and spill from my eyes. "I've never needed a man, never given my heart to anyone until you. We can work it out. You can travel and I'll be busy with my investigations. There's email and texting, and you have to come back sometimes to check in with Dylan and Carina."

"Those are the physical arrangements. I can do all those things, but my heart, Kelly, I have no heart to give to you. I'll just be taking from you, feeding off your kindness. I can't give you what you need."

~ Tyler ~

Tyler stood in the shadows outside the sanctuary, waiting for the regular attenders to enter the church. He pulled his hood over his face and shivered in the chill of the evening.

Families, large and small, gathered around the foyer, greeting each other and chatting happily. Children darted between the adults, chasing and playing tag. His heart lumped into his throat at the joy and anticipation everyone had for the children's program.

A security guard patrolled the perimeter of the building. Tyler stepped behind a columnar Italian cypress tree, glad he had had the foresight to wear camouflage.

He shouldn't be here, but he couldn't bear not seeing Kelly and Bree. Even though he couldn't play an active role in their lives, he'd always carry them in his heart and pray for them.

"Baa, baa, baa," a little girl's voice made Tyler jump.

It was Bree, dressed in her fluffy white sheep costume made of curly yarn and glued-on cotton balls. Floppy ears hung over her blond curls, and her nose was painted into a black dot.

She ran, screaming 'baa,' chased by a shepherd boy.

Tyler skulked behind the row of trees, his heart pounding, his senses on full alert.

Bree swung around the end of the row and shrieked as the boy tagged her. "Gotcha, you're it."

Laughing and giggling, Bree turned on the boy and yelled, "Baa, baa, baa."

Tyler blew out a breath of relief, but his heart was still beating too fast. He'd better pull himself together. There were no threats here. Again, he scanned the checkpoints, noting the cars entering the driveway and the people filing toward the church auditorium.

Where was Kelly? How could she let Bree run around where she could get hit by a car or snatched by perverts? The sole security guard was useless. He waved his flashlight aimlessly and seemed more interested in flirting with the young women than watching for danger.

Tyler stalked the children, keeping himself low and in the shadows of the wall and trees. A Sunday school teacher blew a whistle and corralled the children into the multipurpose room. Meanwhile, the adults set up their video cameras and tripods.

Kelly, her mother Peggy, Ella, and Jaden hustled past Tyler. He caught a glimpse of Kelly's face. Her skin was paler than usual, and she was silent. Jaden and Ella cracked jokes and seemed to go out of their way to make Kelly smile, but when she did, her eyes remained serious.

"Hey, you need any help?" The rent-a-cop slapped his baton on his palm. "The hot meals are in the morning, if that's what you're looking for."

"Actually, I'm here to worship." Tyler shrugged. "Just making sure the women and elderly have enough chairs to sit. I can stand on the side."

"Okay, we're closing the doors. It's the Christmas Pageant, so we're keeping interruptions to a minimum."

Tyler slid into the auditorium and parked himself in the corner hidden by the large flag behind the piano. He'd get a good view of the stage, but stay out of sight of the congregation.

The lights were dimmed after the pastor's welcome and prayer, so Tyler settled on the steps leading to the choir gallery.

Parents crowded around him with their video cameras and cell phone cameras. Fortunately, Jaden was taking the video, and he seemed oblivious to Tyler's presence.

The play started with the shepherds standing on a patch of artificial turf. Sheep pranced and frolicked. Tyler's heart warmed at the sight of Bree as she scampered, yelling her one line "Baa" at the top of her lungs with the same exuberance she'd once asked him to throw her into the air and catch her.

Three shepherds waddled with their staves, made a half-hearted attempt at herding the sheep, then sat on the turf. From the left side of the stage came three wise men who were actually boys dressed in long robes. They wore turbans and false beards.

The spotlight trained on a boy wearing a crown. It was King Herod. His robe was well stuffed. He patted his chest and proclaimed. "I order you to find the baby and bring me word."

"Yes, your majesty," one of the wise men said. They turned and walked off the stage.

The boy with the crown swaggered around, holding his bulging robe. "Ha, ha, ha. I will kill all the baby boys in Judea. Not one shall escape."

He shifts the bombs under his robe and holds up his hands. There's a detonator! He's going to blow. Unlike the other boy, this one's smiling. He's taunting the shepherds and sheep. "You die. You all die."

I can't shoot. He's only a boy. I lunge at him. I don't care if I die too. I grab his wrist and twist his arm behind his back and search his vest for the bombs. They're hidden behind white pillows.

The villagers scream and shout. All the shepherds flee, leaving their sheep who run after them crying. One of the sheep comes to thank me for saving her.

"Tyler, Tyler." A female soldier grabs me from behind. She throws the water from her canteen at me.

"Kelly?" Tyler's eyes grew wide. What was going on? A stampede of church members filed for the exits. From the side, the rent-a-cop approached, his billy club pointed at Tyler, as if he were a rabid dog.

"Calm, calm," the guard said. "Put your hands up against the wall."

"Don't hit him," Kelly said. "He needs help. He's a veteran."

"Ty!" Bree ran toward him right in front of the guard who took a swipe with his club.

Tyler scooped Bree out of the way and pushed out the side door. Cold air slammed into his lungs. He swung Bree over his shoulders and sprinted for the row of trees.

"You'll be safe with me. No one's going to hurt you. No one."

"Whee!" Bree said. "Throw me higher."

"No time, sweetie. Got to get away from the enemy."

"Tyler, Tyler." Kelly's voice carried from the building. "Come back with Bree. Tyler, please."

"Save Mama too," Bree said. "I want Mama."

Tyler snapped his head around. Lights were trained on him. Kelly held out her arms. "I can help you. Let me help you."

"No." He put Bree down. "I don't need you. I don't need anyone."

Drawing his hood over his face, he vaulted over the cinder block wall and sprinted down the alley. Sirens rang in the distance as he scrambled down the stairs of the BART station. He had enough on his fare card to take him across the Bay.

There'd be a manhunt. Charges filed. The child was not a suicide bomber; he was playing King Herod.

They'd say he tried to kidnap Bree. His darling Bree who wasn't afraid of him, who trusted him. They'd turn her against him. Tell her he was a crazy vet. Someone to be pitied. Not good enough to be normal.

He arrived at the West Oakland BART station without being detained. No one cared about a single homeless man, one dressed in camouflage fatigues. Invisible, to be shunned and avoided.

Tyler crossed under the busy interstate and hopped a fence into the railyard harboring rows and rows of freight trains. One was slowly pulling out of the station.

With one easy leap, he pulled himself into an empty boxcar covered with graffiti. The train picked up speed, rattling to its destination to points unknown. Tyler sat against the wall and put his head between his knees.

God, forgive me. Take this worthless man and do with me what you can. I give up. I need help. I need You.

Chapter 21

~ Kelly ~

"HE CAN'T HAVE JUST VANISHED." I pace back and forth in front of Tyler's friend, Sawyer. We're in the Oakland BART station following up on a tip.

"No one here's seen him so far. Is he answering his phone?"

"Of course not. His battery must be dead by now."

It's been two days since Tyler disappeared.

"Hold on," Sawyer says. He approaches a man meditating on a blanket.

"Yo, Raj."

The thin, bearded man ignores him.

Sawyer bends with his hands on his knees and blows in the man's face.

The man's eyes snap open, and it takes a moment before they focus with recognition. "Sawyer? Tom Sawyer?"

"Sawyer McGee. But I'm not here for yoga lessons. It's about G.I. Joe. You seen him?"

"G.I. Joe? Army man?" Raj scratches his head, then scratches his armpits. "Little green Army men."

"Not little. Real guy. My homie, Tyler Manning."

"Yes, he's wearing green camouflage. Not desert gray. It was green jungle."

"That's him." Sawyer snaps his fingers. "Think, think. He get off or get on. Which train?"

"He got off. Cold night. Drizzling. Headed toward the train yards. He asked me which way to go. I told him."

Sawyer slips a fiver to Raj. "Good job, man. You see him again you tell me."

"Not going to see him. He said goodbye. Have a nice life, and the next life after. He's gone. I saw into his soul, gray aura, death."

I shudder as a chill creeps over my shoulders and wraps around my scalp. "Tyler wouldn't kill himself, would he?"

Sawyer takes my arm. "Nah, he's too strong for that. He's probably taking a vacation. Going to see the sights. I bet he's headed to Colorado. His family used to have a farm there."

"Did he tell you about it? Do you know where? What town?"

"No idea. Sorry. He only talked about it in general."

It's times like this I wish I had a smartphone and a browser. "I don't have a clue where he's from."

"Know anyone who knew him back then? Any former girlfriends? High school sweethearts?"

I hang my head. "He never talked about anyone other than an uncle who had a tree farm. Of course his parents are gone."

"We could put out an ad or contact the press."

"No, Tyler would hate the publicity." I've already stopped the church from going public. After Tyler's episode, I held a meeting with the congregation, telling them Tyler's story, minus the part about killing the boy. Everyone agreed to keep it out of the press and to pray for him.

I try his phone again, but my call goes directly to voicemail. "Let me call my sister. Maybe she can do some research on the internet. I want to find him before Christmas."

"Good luck. He could be anywhere." Sawyer shakes his head. "I heard there's a blizzard descending over the Rockies. If I were him, I would have gone south to Mexico."

~ *Tyler* ~

Tyler huddled in the rear cutout of a grain hopper he'd caught at Salt Lake City. Snow blew through the opening, and a freezing wind pummeled him.

The first day was relatively smooth crossing through Sacramento and into Nevada. But when the freight train stopped in Salt Lake City, Tyler had jumped off. He'd bought a parka, snow boots, gloves, sleeping bag and backpack from a secondhand store, then skulked around the yard waiting for a train headed east.

He'd finally caught this one headed for Denver, which meant it had to go near his boyhood town right outside of Grand Junction.

Tyler tucked himself into the waterproof sleeping bag. Gingerly, he fumbled through his backpack and counted his money. Twenty dollars and change left from his advance. He still had the smartphone, but he'd have to mail it back. He itched to turn it on and let Kelly know he was okay, but with the fancy tracking devices, he couldn't risk it.

His chest ached at the disappointment and embarrassment he'd caused Kelly. That hurt look on her face while she'd pleaded with him. *I can help you. Let me help you.*

Did she even know what it would take to help a man like him? Had she a clue how he'd drain all the happiness out of her life? Deplete her until she had nothing left to give? Suck the life out of her?

The outlook for veterans with PTSD, especially ones who had lucid flashbacks and outbursts was grim, and Tyler didn't want to saddle anyone with his nightmare.

The miles rattled by as Tyler dozed off and on. Near evening, the train slowed and entered the Grand Junction railyard, the hub of transportation for the fruits and agricultural products grown in the fertile Grand Valley.

Tyler kept his eyes peeled for the rail cops and waited until his car was in between parallel rows of boxcars. Once the train was barely above walking speed, Tyler hefted his backpack and bag and hopped off. He took a bathroom break and zigzagged between tracks to get out of the yard.

"Hey you," a man yelled through a bullhorn in his white pickup truck. He gunned the accelerator and drove straight at Tyler.

Tyler scrambled over a flat car, then ran the opposite direction. With a mile of freight train between them, he cut several banks of tracks and climbed up an embankment. Fort Manning, Colorado was only a few miles north.

~ *Kelly* ~

I'm on my way to Fort Manning, after flying into Grand Junction on a puddle jumper from Phoenix. It's after five and the sun is setting.

"There are only two motels and I'm not sure they're even open this time of year. Sure you don't want to stay in Grand Junction?" the cab driver asks as we drive past a chain motel on the interstate.

"No, I'll figure it out when I get there."

"Okay, don't say I didn't warn you," the driver said. "When we get there, I'll stick around and get a cup of coffee in case you change your mind."

"Thanks, that's nice of you. Actually, I'd like you to take me to the local cemetery after I get a room."

"It'll be dark, ma'am. You sure you know what you're doing?" He turns and stares at me over his shoulder.

"I'm meeting someone out there."

His eyes bug out, and he makes the sign of the cross, before turning his attention back to the road.

I'm surprised how flat it is out here. I always thought of Colorado as mountainous. Instead, the snow barely dusts the ground, and flat top mesas loom in the distance.

The road gets narrower as we ascend toward one of the mesas. The snow covered rock walls gleam ghostly over the red earth. A gas station and two small buildings sit at a crossroads. One of them is boarded up, and the other is hidden under a pile of snow.

"This is it," the driver says. "I'd ask at the gas station which one is open, but then again, it's a coin toss."

~ *Tyler* ~

Tyler trekked the remaining miles on foot after hitching a ride with a farmer. When Tyler told the man he was going to Fort Manning, the old farmer had said, "Mannings never give up. Too bad there aren't any more Mannings left in these parts."

Tyler rubbed his cold hands and cut through a field, skipping the single crossroad in town near the highway. Back at Grand Junction, he'd filled his backpack with food and bought a wreath, but he didn't dare show his face in the small town, especially one named for his ancestors.

He headed for the old cabin in the canyon. The buyers for their farm hadn't wanted the dilapidated shack, so his mother had kept it under his name.

After hiking several miles following a dry gully, he reached the old shack. Snow covered the roof in patches and the stone structure was still standing, but he was sure there'd be leaks. He found the key in its hiding place under the porch. There would be no electricity or running water. After stowing his things, he took the wreath and hiked to the abandoned cemetery.

The gravestones were covered with mud. Using a stick, Tyler cleared the stones until his parents' names appeared.

"I'm truly alone in this world."

I'll always be your hero, son. He heard his father's voice in his mind.

I'll always pray for you, Tyler. His mother's voice played across the breeze.

"I belong here, with you. There's nothing out there for me."

You're a hero, son. Don't let me down.

He traced his father's name on the headstone.

You're a man who'll be one lucky woman's world.

And he placed the wreath under his mother's name.

"But I'm still alone. I have to be."

Alone with God is never alone, a still, small voice whispered in the wind.

Be brave, my son.

Mannings never give up.

Tears rolled down Tyler's face. *There will be no Mannings left in these hills. There will be nobody to heal the wounds left by war. No laughter, no smiles, no hope if I fail my mission.*

He rose from his knees and kissed the stone. *Goodbye, Father. Farewell, Mother. I'll see you across the Jordan, in that bright and shining land.*

Chapter 22

~ Kelly ~

"ANY ONE OF YOU BRAVE men want to take me to the Fort Manning cemetery?" I wave a twenty-dollar bill at the two yokels eating chips and drinking beer at the gas station.

The driver claims he's afraid of ghosts, that he has no snow chains, and his wife's expecting a baby. Oh, and he has to pee.

The guy with the beard belches and scratches his belly. "Ain't no cemetery. That's a family plot behind the abandoned fort."

"They say there's ghosts up there." The other guy picks his nose and studies his finger. "Some kid took his girlfriend to the fort, and I'm telling you, something happened and they ain't the same anymore."

I pull out another twenty. "Let me borrow your truck if you're too chicken."

The bearded guy scoops up the money. "Let's go, but don't say I didn't warn you."

The cab driver comes out of the bathroom. "You want me to wait?"

"Nah, you go ahead," the bearded guy says. "I'll take care of her."

"Okie doke." The little man bobs his head and skedaddles back to his cab.

We get into the bearded guy's rusty truck, and it starts after he cranks it a few times.

"Who you looking for?" He spits out the window. "Baby daddy knock you up or what?"

"You haven't seen a guy wearing camouflage around these parts, have you?"

"Should have asked before you gave me the money. Truth is, we ain't seen nobody." He turns the truck off the pavement onto a bumpy dirt track covered with snow. "It gets dark out here real early. You don't want to go wandering off."

"I won't."

"The last few yards is walking only. I'm staying with the truck."

So much for taking care of me.

"It's okay. I won't be long."

"You're crazy going out there by yourself."

"Just drive, will you?"

For the next several miles he's silent, but as we drive between a narrow crevice and down into a canyon, he turns to me.

"Lots of varmints out there. You don't want to run into a cougar."

"I'm big enough to handle it." I stare out the window at the deepening shadows. If Tyler's out there, I have to find him and let him know I still care for him.

"How much he owe you?" The guy just won't shut up. "I mean you don't come out here unless you want something."

"I'm looking for Tyler Manning, you know him?"

The guy throws his head back and laughs. "Every one of them was named Tyler Manning. From the old General to the young one. They'd be lots of ghosts answering to Tyler Manning."

"I'm looking for the young one."

"The one who went batshit crazy? You won't find him here. You'll be lucky to find the grave stones."

"Well, thanks a lot for the encouragement, Mr. what did you say your name was again?"

"I didn't say. And there it is." He idles at the end of the road. A rusted chain is attached to two rotting fence posts.

"Out you go," the man says. "I'm not staying here all night. If I have to go in looking for you, you owe me favors."

I slam the door with a resounding rattle. Tyler's got to be out there. I can feel it.

"Half hour," the man's voice trails after me. "Give me your cell number in case you get lost."

"I won't get lost. Tyler will show me the way." I don't know why I'm feeling crazy, even fey, but the man jumps from his truck and strides toward me.

"Give me your number. I'm not going to be responsible for some fancy city woman disappearing out here."

"Fine, if only to let you know I'm okay." I dictate my number to him. "Thanks."

He texts me a moment later so I have his number.

A chill skitters its way down my spine as I walk into the wilderness. Darkness falls fast between the buttes and canyon walls. I follow a trackless trail along the wire fence. There are no fresh footprints. If Tyler's been here, he didn't come this way.

The trail gets smaller, and I'm not sure if I'm going the right way. I pull back the tree branches along the broken down fence and feel my way into a small clearing. I can barely make out the rock hewn ruins of the old fort.

The cemetery or family plot has to be close by. My heartbeat flails when I see footprints. He's here. What will I say to him? He'll think I'm crazy to come after him. He'll run from me.

But I didn't come this far to turn back. Hitching my breath, I swing my arms and jog in the direction of the tracks. It's not snowing, and the tracks are still fresh.

I follow them around the corner of a broken wall and stop short. Among the lumps of snow covered headstones are two wiped clean. A wreath is propped under one of them.

"Tyler." I rush to the gravesites, but he's not there. His departing footsteps disappear toward the ravine beyond.

I'm too late.

"Tyler! Wait up. Tyler." I can barely make out the footprints in the dusk. I quicken my steps into a loping running pace.

After several twists and turns where I'm unsure if I'm on his trail or not, I crash through a thicket of scrawny trees and find an old stone cabin.

I run to the door. "Tyler, it's me, Kelly."

~ Tyler ~

Tyler put his thumb down and jogged up to the eighteen-wheeler.

"How far are you going?" he asked the driver, a stout bald guy.

"Salt Lake City. Hop on. I need someone to keep me awake."

"Sure thing, buddy." Tyler pulled himself into the rig.

"Something tells me you got a story." The man shuts off the radio. "You going home for Christmas?"

"Yep, going home."

"Where's that?"

"I left my heart in San Francisco." Tyler leaned back in the captain's chair. Hitchhiking sure beat jumping trains.

The driver, Charlie Foster, turned out to be a Vietnam veteran. Tyler had never met one before.

"Yep, we're a dying breed," Charlie said. "But we survived. Ever been a prisoner?"

"No, sir."

"Then you're lucky." Charlie pats his belly. "I was ninety-eight pounds when they released me from the Hanoi Hilton."

"You must have seen some horrible sights."

"Not just seen, been them. Had my bones sticking out of my leg. Buddy's brains splattered all over me when he got fragged. A man never gets over them."

"But how do you cope? I get flashbacks so real. Problem with Afghanistan, there weren't marked battlefields where we fought. We patrolled and everywhere we went, something could go wrong. I can never relax."

"You ever freak out? Go on a rampage because you think you're back there?"

"Yeah, I do." Tyler hung his head. "That's why I ran. It's like nothing helps. I take my meds, I go to therapy, but everything comes back crystal clear and poof, I'm back there."

"You need a circuit breaker," Charlie said. "Just like something triggers the flashback, you need something to step you back."

"Like slapping myself? I never remember to pinch or slap."

"No, a stop word or phrase, like 'Snickerdoodles' or 'Taj Mahal.' It's like hitting the pause button and then your conscious mind can take over. Right now, it's all emotions, your heart beating, sweating, adrenaline pumping."

"I wish it were so simple."

"Nothing simple at all. But it might help to get a mentor, because your wife and kids?" Charlie jerked his thumb back at the family pictures pinned to the back of his cab. "They won't understand. Don't expect them to. You call your mentor, and he talks you off the ledge. He's been there. He knows what you're going through, and he won't leave you in the foxhole alone. Find a guy at your local veteran's group. I can hook you up with one of my buddies who lives near you."

"Thanks, I will." Tyler glanced at the family pictures. "How do you keep them happy when you're falling apart?"

"Tell yourself, this too will pass. This too will pass. Then appreciate the hell out of them. That's all you can do. You're not here to make their lives perfect. You're here to share your life with them."

"I have so much I want to do. So many things I need to accomplish."

"There's nothing stopping you, brother." Charlie said. "Nothing but your own fears. Let them go."

"I'm trying. Believe me, I'm trying. I tell myself, no more running. There's someone I want to make a life with. Someone special."

Charlie gave him a thumbs up. "I knew it. You had that look in your eye."

He turned on the radio and "I'll be Home for Christmas" played on the air.

The miles rolled on. Tyler couldn't keep Kelly and Bree from his mind. When it was time to say goodbye to Charlie, Tyler had made a decision. He'd be the best man he could for Kelly and the best father in the world for Bree. *Thank you, God, for sending Charlie my way.*

He hopped from the cab and reached for his cell phone. It wasn't in any of his pockets.

~ Tyler ~

It was the day before Christmas when Tyler arrived back in San Francisco. None of the people he met on the road seemed to take special notice of him, and there was nothing on the radio about a manhunt for a veteran.

He double-checked his surroundings and took a quick shower at the Y. His street friends were not in their usual spots, and he hadn't seen Sawyer at the BART station. Of course, now that he had the gig with Jewell's band, he no longer needed to busk.

Tyler wandered into an electronics store and watched the news on the TV screens while last minute shoppers snapped up gifts. He browsed the internet and googled his name. There was no mention of the incident at Pacific Baptist Church. Nothing at all about his disappearance.

How did that happen? He could have sworn the police sirens were after him.

The latest news on him showed him at the Warspring Donor's Ball wearing a Santa hat and holding hands with Kelly. He couldn't take his eyes off her image. She was simply stunning. Her dress was not revealing like the rest of the women's. Everything about her was clean and fresh. She looked like an executive, with a sharp gaze and confident chin, but so feminine she made his toes curl.

Walking back into her life wasn't going to be easy. He couldn't just go knocking on her mother's door. Not after the scene at the church.

Tyler retraced his steps to the Ferry Building. The sun was out, but the temperature was low enough for hats and mittens.

The outdoor ice skating rink glistened in front of a row of palm trees under the clock tower. Long lines of children snaked around the block. Tyler made his way across the plaza and leaned against the barricade to see if he could spot Kelly and Bree.

He had to chuckle at the Californian skaters. Many of them hugged the walls, and others were so wobbly they fell more than they skated. And then there were the macho teen boys who raced out of control on hockey skates but went barreling into the walls.

Not a way to impress a girl, buddy. Maybe for laughs.

Several fellows pretended they were playing hockey, more like air hockey since they had no sticks. Out of the corner of his eye, he spied a tall, thin man with a hockey bag arguing with an attendant about their 'no stick' policy.

Tyler put his hands in his pockets and suppressed the urge to react. *Not my fight. Not my monkeys.*

He walked around the rink. Could that little blond girl be Bree? He edged his way closer, but the woman holding her hand was shorter and had spiked hair under her earmuffs. Not Kelly.

The man who had argued with the attendant was lacing up his hockey skates. He still had his hockey bag looped over his shoulder. When he passed through the barricade onto the ice, he slipped a long dark object out of his bag.

The man raises an AR-15 assault weapon with a fully loaded magazine. He waves it around at the skaters who are oblivious. No one sees what he's doing.

I leap silently over the barricade and sneak up on him. No sense alarming the crowd. The man zeroes in on his target.

It's Bree. Bree's twirling out on the ice. Her silvery blond hair flies in the air. She's giggling and laughing.

The man steadies his aim, and I pounce.

Boom. Boom. Boom. He squeezes off several rounds. I'm rolling on the slippery ice. My heart is on overdrive, thumping. Did anyone get hurt? Screams rend the air and people are panicking.

The bastard won't let go of the semi-automatic. He pulls the trigger, and the blast deafens me. I can't let him shoot anyone else. I just can't. I pound on him, gouge his eyes, and knee him in the gut.

It all comes down to me to get the rifle away from him. Man to man, hand to hand. I won't let him go. He tried to shoot Bree. He tried to kill her. I slam his head on the ice. He drops the AR-15, and I grab it.

"Hands up. Police." Gruff voices shout behind me, and rough hands yank me from the bloodied man.

Chapter 23

~ Kelly ~

A POLICEMAN ESCORTS ME TOWARD the San Francisco Police Station. Ella and Bree are in there, and so is Tyler.

No one knows exactly what happened, except some man pulled an assault rifle at the ice rink. I don't believe it's Tyler, but the police are holding him because he was the one with the rifle when they arrived on the scene.

They assure me no one was shot, although reports vary on how many shots were fired.

"Step back, step back." The officers cordon a path for me up the steps. They lead me past the reception area and down a long corridor.

One officer knocks briefly on the door and ushers me into an office. Bree is sitting on the window ledge, and Ella's speaking to the officer behind the desk.

"Mama!" Bree jumps off the ledge and slams into me. "Ty saved my life. I almost got shot!"

"Bree." I hug her and kiss her. Tears stream down my face at how I could have lost her. "Ella, what happened? What was Tyler doing?"

"I didn't see it," she says, her voice shaking. I only saw the flash and I grabbed Bree and ran. We slipped and fell, and everyone was falling or crawling to get away."

I reach over and fold her and Bree into my arms. We hold each other, trembling and crying. After we calm down, I ask if I can see Tyler.

"No visitors. He's being held for questioning."

"But he didn't do it, did he? He'd never do something like this."

"We're analyzing all the witnesses' statements as well as forensics. You can take your daughter and sister home. They were very fortunate." He leads us to the door. "Oh, and Merry Christmas."

~ *Kelly* ~

We celebrate Christmas Eve at my mother's apartment. Jaden and Ella, me and Bree. No one talks about Tyler. Mother had made us promise not to dampen our spirits with his troubles.

As far as I know, he's still being held on weapons charges. Discharging an assault weapon is a serious offense, and it being the holidays means no judge is going to move on granting him bail.

The guy Tyler tackled is the son of a billionaire, the idiot who gave me the bad stock tip. Rebecca was right. He'd traded the opposite way, wiped me out, then got a slap on the wrist, no jail time thanks to daddy dearest.

This time, he's not getting away, even if the press is going around pegging Tyler as the one going nuts and the billionaire's son as the innocent bystander.

I'm praying someone captured the event on video. Somewhere out there is a film that will exonerate Tyler. I'm in no mood to celebrate, but for Bree's sake, I pull on a happy face.

We go through the motions, singing carols, giving thanks, and opening our one gift for Christmas Eve. Bree chooses the gift Tyler and I bought the day we met at the Ferry Building.

"A monster kit," she squeals. "I wanna make one and show Ty. He's coming, isn't he? After they let him out of jail."

"Let's make one and put it under the tree for him." I know I shouldn't feed her dreams, but my heart aches because it's what I want more than ever.

"Yay, Santa pwo-mised. He did." Bree lifts her chin, so assured in her beliefs. "I also asked God to be safe."

"So did I." I kiss the top of her head.

Ella puts her arm over my shoulder. "Let's all pray for Tyler."

Several hours later, I'm finally able to relax. It took some bribing, lots of cookies and warm milk, including a share for Santa, and not a few threats about Santa not coming down the chimney at houses where children stayed up, before Bree was satisfied to go to sleep.

Mother went to bed soon after Bree. Ella and Jaden left to spend Christmas at Jaden's parents' house, leaving me alone and awake.

I heat two mugs of apple cider and add a splash of whiskey. Setting one on the kitchen table across from me, I cradle mine and sip, imagining Tyler and me kicking back and sharing a laugh.

Either I must have dozed off, or the knocking was faint and I'd imagined it. My heartbeat quickens as I pad to the door. "Is anyone there?"

"Ho, ho, ho, Santa Claus here." It's Tyler's voice.

I fling open the door. Tyler stands there with a large bag over his shoulder.

Joy springs from my heart, and I throw myself into his arms. "They let you out. I knew you didn't do it."

He drops the bag, and his mouth swoops down to capture mine. Relief and elation flood through me as I shower him with kisses.

I drag him into the apartment. "Tell me everything. What happened? How did they let you out?"

"Whoa, whoa, whoa." He presses a finger on my lips. "First, I have to put all the presents under the tree. Then I eat the cookies Bree left for me, and then, I get a kiss under the mistletoe."

"You got your kiss already." I laugh. "Okay, let me help."

Tyler drags a box out of the bag. It's a Christmas train set. "For Bree."

"She'll love it." I arrange the rest of the presents while he builds the train tracks around the Christmas tree.

While we assemble the track and trains, he tells me how he'd gone to his parents' graves, how he met a Vietnam veteran who hooked him up with a veteran's group, and how the police had let him go after a video was turned in showing Tyler as the guy who stopped the shooting.

"That means you're the hero. You saved Bree and everyone else." I hug him. "The shooter was the guy who gave me the bad trade. Even though he didn't go to jail, he had to pay back all his winnings and a huge fine. His father cut off his allowance, and he probably blames it on me for getting caught."

Tyler's lips press tight and he nods. "I'll never let anyone hurt you or Bree. Not if I can help it."

I swallow a tight lump in my throat. Of course he'd never let anyone hurt me or Bree physically, but he could still damage our hearts. Should I risk it? Put myself out there? Does he even know I went after him?

I light the gas fireplace and drop pillows on the carpet in front of the Christmas tree. Getting comfortable, I lean into his arms.

"Tyler, I trust you with my life and know you won't let anyone else hurt me, but what about you? When you left, it hurt really, really bad. I can take it, but I don't want Bree to ever feel abandoned."

"I feel horrible leaving you like that." He presses a kiss on my forehead. "I was afraid to ruin your life. It's not going to be easy being with me."

"It's not easy being with anyone." I stroke his forearm and take his hand. "We all have our baggage, and there's no guarantee of the future. That's why I never wanted a relationship. I thought I could raise Bree by myself, shield her from pain and rejection."

He caresses my shoulders and back, holding me close. "Has someone hurt you? Rejected you?"

The lump in my throat grows and I nod. “My father has another family. What you see here are the castoffs. Me, my mother, and my sister. When my mother got sick, he didn’t lift a finger to help us. When I went to jail, he disinherited me. He tried to manipulate Ella. Made her choose between his money and us.”

“She chose wisely. And so do I.” He tilts my chin to face him. “I need you, Kelly. I won’t ever run off without talking to you.”

“You better not. After I went all the way to Colorado to find you.”

His eyes widen, and his jaw slackens. “You followed me? What happened when you didn’t find me?”

“I froze my tush in your cabin until the guy I hired to take me to the old fort came and got me. He must have felt sorry for me because he drove me straight to the airport and made me get on the plane. Call it temporary insanity.”

He sweeps my hair from my face. “I prefer to call it love. I’m sorry I missed you. I was already on my way back to you.”

I bury my face in his neck and hold him, my heart fluttering with warmth and happiness. I’ve reached him. He’s able to feel my love and believe it. Trust me enough to come back and take another chance. But can I trust him?

Tyler caresses my hair and whispers, “You’re incredible. I can’t believe you were there.”

“Oh, believe me, I had to put up with some real characters at your hometown.” I take his hand and intertwine my fingers with his. “I saw your footsteps and your parents’ graves, the wreath you left, and the little stone cabin in the canyon. I understand why you went.”

“I needed to be with my parents. To feel like I’m not alone in this world. They were there, in my heart. But I needed more than two gravestones. So I came back for you. I couldn’t stay away.” His warm breath brushes over me. “Everything was empty without you. My mother always said

I'd one day be some woman's entire world. I want to be yours."

I reach for his face and gaze into his eyes. They seem truer and bluer than I remember. "Stay with me, and be Bree's father too."

He blinks and wets his lips, a look of hope opening his face. "You trust me?"

"With my heart." I kiss the stubble on his jaw. "And Bree's."

"Let me protect and care for you." He clasps my hands between his strong, warm hands. "You and Bree. Let me be the man in your life."

"You already are. I'm falling in love with you."

"I love you, Kelly, with all my heart."

"Merry Christmas, Tyler."

~ *Tyler* ~

"Nana, Nana, look what Santa got me." Bree's chirpy voice pierced the morning stillness.

Tyler shifted his body on the pillows and cracked his eyes open. The needles of the Christmas tree brushed against his face. Kelly was asleep in his arms, and Bree stood over them, still wearing her pajamas.

Bree tapped Kelly. "Mama, what are you doing with my present?"

"Huh, what?" Kelly yawned and stretched. Her elbow caught Tyler in the jaw.

He rubbed his face. "Ouch. I'm getting assaulted on Christmas morning."

Footsteps shuffled down the hallway. "Bree, it's too early."

"But, Nana, look. Mama and Ty are under the Chwistmas tree. I bet they were kissing." She danced a storm around them, laughing and jumping in glee.

Kelly blushed and straightened her rumpled blouse. Thankfully, they'd fallen asleep fully clothed while cuddling, nothing more.

"Oh, my bones," Peggy said. She stopped at the entrance to the living room. "Well I'll be fit to be darned. Looks like we all got our present under the big ol' tree."

"You, Mama?" Kelly's eyebrow cocked at her mother.

"Oh, yes," she replied. "I asked for a handyman."

"You did not, you asked for a son-in-law."

"Same difference."

"I asked for a papa." Bree landed in Tyler's lap and hugged him.

"And Kelly? What did you ask for?"

"I asked for love, but got you instead." She winked before smacking him with the best Christmas kiss he ever got.

- THE END –

Thank you for reading *A Father for Christmas*. Please consider writing a review if you enjoyed the story.

Sign up for my Newsletter http://bit.ly/RachAyala to keep in touch and get news of upcoming books, projects, and events.

Acknowledgments

First of all, I want to thank Chantel Rhondeau and her friends in the *Killer Romances* boxed set for inspiring me to write a Christmas love story. There's always something magical about the Christmas season that brings miracles into our hearts and joy into our lives. Of course, the true meaning of Christmas is God's undying love for us. He sent His Son as a gift to all mankind.

My awesome beta team has had a lot of reading to do this year, and I thank them from the bottom of my heart. Ruth Davis, Amber McCallister, Joanna Daniel, Chantel Rhondeau, and Shecki Bernard. I had a very short timeframe to turn this around, and they rose to the occasion and gave me their feedback in record time. Thank you, ladies!

My heartfelt thanks to all my readers who've written me and told me they enjoyed my stories. I'm grateful to you for letting me share my stories with you. You keep me inspired.

God gets all the glory, and I'm awed by his provision and care. I'm thankful for my salvation through Jesus Christ.

About the Author

I love the magic of the Christmas season filled with family and the spirit of giving and helping others. From romantic suspense to sweet contemporaries, I write from my heart and love to include children and pets in my stories.

I am grateful that *A Father For Christmas* has won the 2015 Readers' Favorite Gold Award for Christian Romance.

Fiction: *Michal's Window, Broken Build, Hidden Under Her Heart, Chance for Love Boxed Set, Knowing Vera, Taming Romeo, Whole Latte Love, Played by Love, Playing the Rookie, A Father for Christmas, Claiming Carlos, Roaring Hot!, Christmas Flirt, Playing Without Rules, Christmas Stray, Intercepted by Love, Leap Laugh Love, A Pet for Christmas, Christmas Lovebirds, Santa's Pet, Valentine Hound Dog*

Nonfiction: *Your Daily Bible Verse, Romance in a Month, 366 Ways to Know Your Character*

Kelly, Tyler, and Bree's story continues one year later ...

>>><<<

Kelly Kennedy thought her life was finally on track. Engaged to the man of her dreams and with a baby on the way, she reassures her five-year-old daughter, Bree, that the father she picked for Christmas still loves her.

Unfortunately, war veteran Tyler Manning has been away most of the year. Recovering from PTSD isn't easy. Rather than worry Kelly, Tyler spends his time traveling to Afghanistan to work at a children's charity he founded.

Kelly decides to distract Bree with promises of a pet for Christmas. When Tyler is captured by terrorists, she finds it hard to convince Bree that they will truly be a family in time for Christmas.

Made in the USA
Lexington, KY
08 August 2019